7 Days til Dawn

debi pysell

Tate Publishing, LLC.

ISBN: **1-5988643-9-4**

Dedication

This book is dedicated to Dr. Barb Eichler,
who encouraged me to write.

Acknowledgement

I would like to thank Angel Mirza, who inadvertently gave me an idea; Rose VanMersbergen, who aided me in seeing that idea through; and to Mary Schulz and Gary Betts, for helping me turn that idea into a reality.

Chapter 1

Elizabeth Simmons was only twenty-seven and had everything to live for. She was beautiful, talented, and kind-hearted. She had a wonderful family and a loving, successful boyfriend that she visited nearly every weekend in Chicago. She felt that the world was just one big opportunity, and therefore, there was never a need to get upset or held down by any one isolated incident. She had a home in Dallas, but still shared a high-rise condominium in downtown Chicago with her soon-to-be fiancé. Being held down by him was not a disturbing consideration to Elizabeth. In fact, she rather enjoyed the idea of it. In her mind, being with Josh made her feel more alive, more liberated than she would ever feel while being apart from him. Her future was so full of possibilities, so full of wonder that she could virtually feel each and every glorious morning as she awoke. Who would have ever thought that her life would come to such an unspeakable end at such a young age?

Chapter 2

Wednesday Morning

Janice Cloud must have hit her alarm clock at least four times, but it still persisted going off. She knew she had to get up sometime; it was just that the present time would not have been the preference.

As she slowly arose out of bed and got ready for the day's tasks, her cell phone started to ring. Janice reluctantly picked up the phone. "Hello?" she asked blandly.

"Hey Janice," said the voice over the phone, "it's Vivian. Did I wake you?"

"No," she yawned. "What's up?"

"Nothing, just seeing if you're going to pick me up or if you want me to meet you at the house."

She rapidly sat up, "What? When? What time is it?"

"Don't worry, babe, you've got an hour or so. We don't have to meet Sharon until eleven for lunch."

"Oh, yea." The adrenaline began to subside inside of her as she steadily remembered her obligation. "Sharon. How long's she gonna be in town?"

"She leaves Monday. So, you want me to meet you, or what?"

"Yea, no, I'll come get you. When do you get off work?"

"Whenever you get here," Vivian replied with a giggle,

trying to subtly let her friend know that she needed to get moving.

"I'll be there in a half hour," Janice answered. She hung up the phone and turned on the water for a shower.

XXXXX

As she pulled into Vivian's work, Janice noticed a black Viper parked in one of the reserved visitor parking spots. *It must be Sharon's car,* she thought. From what Janice understood, Sharon was a spoiled rich girl who was "between careers" and living on her parents' inheritance. That is, if what she had been doing before could in fact be considered a career. According to her brother, Joshua Surf, she had held a job, data processing, for approximately two weeks before her supervisor kindly asked her to leave. "She took it as a compliment" Joshua had told Janice, not holding back his amusement. "She stated that she had done everything so well that the company no longer needed anyone to do that particular job ever again." *Could anyone in this day and age still be that naïve,* thought Janice. Unfortunately, Vivian Shlimon and Janice Cloud, who were the same ages as Sharon, had been assigned the duty of taking her out to lunch to make her feel more comfortable while she'd be here visiting Joshua. He had stated previously that he didn't have the time to see Sharon during this visit. *Who could honestly blame him though,* thought Janice. *Sharon must be a handful.*

As she pulled up closer to the front of the building, Janice saw Vivian and Joshua Standing just outside the front door.

"Hi Viv, you ready?" Janice asked as she rolled down her window.

"Yea, coming," a faint voice replied. There she was again, flirting with Joshua. It made Janice wonder just how he felt about her friend. She hoped he wasn't just stringing Vivian along in order to get her to do favors (like taking his sister, Sharon, out, for instance) for him.

As Vivian got into the car, Janice figured she'd just find out what she wanted to know. "Did he ask you out yet?" Janice bluntly asked Vivian with a reserved smile. Vivian fumbled with her seatbelt. "No," came a blushing response, "not yet."

As the two girls headed towards the restaurant, Sharon

couldn't help but wonder why Vivian consistently pursued Joshua when she could literally have gotten any guy she wanted . . . *but not him.* God only knew what was going through that guy's head. He constantly but shrewdly turned her down time and again in a way that was just gentle enough to keep her hopeful. Personally, Janice thought he was a player, and he was playing Vivian. The problem with that philosophy was the age-old saying that you "can't play a player."

XXXXX

Elizabeth didn't ever enjoy the feeling of having to lie, even for the people she loved. She felt distressed as she tried to peacefully explain her point of view.

"But when can this end? I'm practically family," Elizabeth pleaded over the phone. "Yes, of course I understand, but . . ." Silence. "Yes. I suppose you're right. I'll be fine," she skeptically stated. "No . . . really. Yes. I'll see you tonight." With her long, brown, plush coat dangling over her left arm, she replaced the phone onto its receiver and turned around. Picking up the round-trip ticket to Chicago, she carefully slid it into her Gucci purse. She felt frustrated and excited at the same time. She was excited about visiting Josh, and frustrated about the way he introduced her to everyone, including his family. *When will this end,* she wondered. She was a vibrant young girl in her late twenties; ready to finally settle in and become something. The problem was that she didn't know what the something was, or who that someone would be that she wanted so badly to become. But she knew beyond a doubt that Josh had to be a part of her life. How long before she would be known to his world for who she was? She longed to be known as his companion, his love, and soon his wife. Did she really have to move to Chicago, now, in order for his friends and family to take her seriously? Couldn't they understand that long-distance relationships are still relationships? Did she have to give up her life in Texas? Of course, she realized, she had no real life here. She had no career that she necessarily felt the need to pursue, nothing to hold her back, and if she did make the move to Chicago permanent, she would never have to worry about who she would become. Josh would guide her as he always had. She was flying to Illinois practically every weekend. Her entire family was in Chicago as well. Perhaps she could actually consider the change. But not now . . . right now, on this beautiful Wednesday morning, she had a plane to catch.

Chapter 3

Wednesday Afternoon

"I guess I should have offered her a ride," Janice realized verbally as she and Vivian pulled up to their favorite Mexican restaurant. "She was in your building, wasn't she?"

"I didn't see her," Vivian replied nonchalantly. "Look, there's a spot right up front." She pointed anxiously to an empty parking spot near the entrance. Janice parked the car, and they proceeded to go inside.

"May I help you?" asked the tall Hispanic doorman.

"Yes, we have reservations for three at eleven o'clock," Vivian replied.

"And the name is under?" he reiterated.

"Surf. Sharon Surf."

"I am sorry, madams, but Ms. Surf has called to cancel her lunch date with you. She has asked me to forward this message to you," he affirmed as he handed the girls a folded note.

"She has left with me her credit card information; will you two care to have lunch? The reservation is still open."

"Sure, thanks," Said Viv as they got escorted to a booth on the side.

Janice opened the note. "Sorry for the inconvenience, but I had some official business to take care of. Thanks anyway. Enjoy lunch, it's on me!" she read out loud. "And it's signed by her highness, Sharon. Great," Janice continued, "I'll believe this bimbo has 'official business' the day pigs fly".

Viv laughed. "Oh, come on now. She may be my sister-in-law one day!"

"Well, at least we can actually have a pleasant lunch." Janice looked at the menu and decided upon her favorite meal at that restaurant. "Whatcha gonna get?" she asked Vivian, setting the menu aside.

"Oh, I don't know." Viv hesitated. "You order for me."

Same as always, but Janice figured she'd give Viv the chance to pick something out on her own. *Who knows, she might have had a taste for something specific.*

As Janice looked around, she couldn't help but get the nagging feeling that something was just not right. *Joshua's little sister was visiting again, as always. She comes at least once every month, stays a few days at a time, and yet she still says that she knows no one but Joshua . . . and us,* she thought, *and now she blows us off for supposed "official business."* The headache began again. Janice could feel it burrowing into her temples. She motioned for a staff member. "Waiter, could I please get a large water?" Smiling through her growing pain, she said, "I'll bet she's having some kind of affair here in Chicago. If she is, I wonder why she hadn't told anyone about it. Maybe Joshua is the protective, big-brother type," she mumbled out loud. The waiter brought a glass of water to the table.

"Thank you." Janice smiled and picked up the water.

As a young girl, Janice noticed a difference in her compared to the other kids her same age. She saw the world in brilliant colors—literally. When she first noticed that she could see a small hint of color around almost every person she looked at, she just assumed that it was normal; that everyone must see the same colors, just as the grass outside is green or the sky above is blue. As she matured, she found out that, indeed, not everyone did see the colors that projected from all the many places that she saw them. Instead of insisting to her friends and family that they were indeed genuine, she decided to brush it off as her eyes playing tricks on her; like the appearance of a lake of water in the middle of a dry desert. They were the same types of tricks that many artists purposefully drew in collages in order to prove that, given the right lighting and atmosphere, the mind will interpret things through the eyes that are not truly valid.

Later in her life, after accepting the strange colors as being a part of her composition, she began to notice a pattern through each color. When people around her would start to get angry or agitated, the colors protruding from them would slowly turn to a deep red glow. She began to speculate if there was indeed a purpose behind the colors she'd seen all her life. She started to enjoy interpreting and viewing the beauty that she saw everywhere. She attempted to test patterns and enjoy the newfound gift she'd been given. Unfortunately, as she matured into young adulthood, she discovered another unique gift. It was a gift that corresponded with anguish. She began to sense when something was going wrong, like when her neighbor's dog had ran out into the road and was hit by a car. Janice was nowhere near the site of the accident, but in a park on the other side of town. Still, she felt a deep, bitter pain inside of her chest, and a feeling of overpowering loss at the precise moment that the poor animal was hit. As time persisted on, those behaviors intensified. She was reluctant to tell anyone about the notions for fear of being labeled psychotic, so she kept them to herself for many years. Then one day, she shared her ability with her closest and dearest friend, Vivian. To Janice's surprise and relief, Vivian did not show any contempt at her friend's competence in feeling other people's losses. Janice never did—and feared she never would—know what to do with this capability. After all, by the time she felt those things and knew that something was wrong, they had already happened; it was too late.

Vivian looked at her friend apprehensively. "Headache again?"

"Yea. I just need some water. You know, just my body telling me to drink more water."

"I hope so. I still think you should see a doctor."

"I have. Many. It's nothing. I just need to take care of myself."

Wherever Sharon was, Vivian and Janice didn't have to deal with her at that time, not until the following day. Sharon's last full day in Chicago, one more dinner with her, then off she was going back home to Texas. *Good riddance.*

XXXXX

"Officer, could you tell me how much longer we have to stay here?"

Steve Spyder turned to see the most beautiful woman he had ever imagined. "Not too much longer, ma'am," he answered as he looked down into her deep blue eyes. Her vibrant smile surrounded a gorgeous set of white teeth, and her long, glowing blonde curls encircled the soft features of her radiant face. "We just need to secure the area for a few more minutes and make sure no one else is hurt. You in a hurry to get somewhere?" he asked with a kind smile.

"No . . . well, yes, I guess. It's OK, really. It's just that I had a meeting over an hour ago, and my plane was already late. I just . . ." Flustered, Sharon smiled back at Steve. "Well, I saw the Elk Grove Police sign over there, and was just wondering if you all will be blocking the exits for long."

"Well, ma'am, we'll be wrapping this up here. If you need a ride . . ."steve demurely asked as he fumbled with his notepad, capping his pen.

Sharon blushed. "Sharon, please. When you call me ma'am, I feel terribly old. Pleasure to meet you." She gave Steve a blossoming smile and extended her right hand. He took the small features of her hand into his own right hand, cupping the top of her delicate fingers with his left. "Steve. Steve Spyder. Pleasure's all mine, and believe me, you have nothing to worry about. You don't look a day over twenty."

"Well, thanks for the compliment, but I'm definitely older than that." Sharon felt a pleasant chill crawl up her spine as the tall, noticeably attractive police officer gently held her hand within both of his. Almost stumbling over her words, Sharon stated, "I'm just visiting relatives. They live here . . . I don't."

Besides the fact that she was stumbling to make a comprehensive sentence, Sharon realized that they had been embracing hands for over a minute. She started to become aware that she was noticeably flushed with an excessive level of attraction towards this mysterious stranger. She quickly removed her hand from his. "I can't . . . I mean I don't need a ride. I'll have a cab waiting for me outside. A friend here has already arranged for it . . . my brother, actually. He's like my friend . . ." She recomposed herself. "Please let me know when I'll be able to leave this side of the airport. I do need to get going." Putting on her coat and gloves, she gave the officer another one of her captivating, warm smiles. "It was very nice meeting you. Thank you for your help; maybe we'll see each other again."

"You can count on it," he said. He gave her a small salute, turned, and started to walk away. Steve felt rejuvenated, full of energy, strong. He turned back toward the chaos blocking one of the exits and thought to himself, *what a way to spend a Wednesday afternoon.*

"OK guys," he stated with a grin as he turned to the other officers, "let's wrap this up"

XXXXX

Lunch was great, as always. Vivian had the chicken enchiladas, and Janice had the veggie burrito. This place was the only Mexican restaurant that they'd ever found that had more than two things on the menu for vegetarians. Janice had always loved Mexican food, but it seemed hard for the restaurants to come up with Mexican vegetarian food that didn't consist entirely of cheese. This place, however, had such a wide variety of avocado, tomato, veggie tacos, veggie burritos, and so many other menu items to choose from that it took Janice almost twenty visits to try everything on the menu for vegetarians. To her, it was amazing, so it was evident why it had become her favorite restaurant.

It was dessert time. Viv and Janice could rarely finish their full meals, let alone dessert, but they repeatedly tried. They usually shared a dessert or two and took about an hour to get it halfway finished, but they enjoyed each other's company.

"Do you have to stop by the developing shop today?" asked Vivian.

"No," Janice answered sarcastically, "but I need to stop in and pick up the paperwork and drop off the deposit tomorrow before dinner with your boyfriend and his lovely sister." Vivian just sat there with that endearing smile on her face, no doubt imagining what it would be like to have Joshua as a boyfriend.

"You could be the photographer at our wedding some day, you know." Vivian slightly came out of her trance and looked toward Janice. "What about you?" she asked. "When are you going to get into the dating schema again?"

"Not for a while." Janice avoided the subject. "So, are you going to go with me to the photo shoots tomorrow?"

"No, I'll meet you after," Viv responded. "What time you gonna be back?"

"Around one. You gonna be able to leave work that early?"

"Yea, Joshua owes me."

Dessert came; it was chocolate mud pie. They both dug in.

Chapter  4

Wednesday Evening

Creeping into Wednesday's night darkness, Sharon's cab dropped her off at the entrance to the condominium. She got out of the car as the driver retrieved her luggage from the trunk. "Your bags, miss. Would you like me to carry them up for you?"

"No, thank you." She handed the driver a tip and with a smile bade him goodnight. She knew that she over-tipped a lot, but she felt that karma would continuously make its rounds. She suddenly felt guilt creep its way into her thoughts. *Was lying to that officer something that karma would eventually justify to me?* Why did she have to start thinking about karma and that remarkable officer? *Steve. What a nice name.* It rolled through her mind quite easily. *Steve. Steve Spyder.*

"Hello, Sharon. Getting in later than usual. I have your keys." Kyle, the doorman, smiled and reached for the set of keys left for her. "Your *brother* left word that he'd be in late. He has your car." The short, endearing, dark-haired doorman handed Sharon her keys with a kind yet perceptive smile. She knew that, although always considerate of her, Kyle held adverse feelings for Joshua. Sharon was a very empathetic person and could understand why Kyle felt that way. He was a perceptive man, and she realized that he was just looking out for her in his own inane way. She looked in his big brown eyes and gave him a pleasing smile.

"Thank you, Kyle. Have a good night."

"Have a good night," he said, returning a sincere smile.

Sharon entered the elevator, still troubled by her desirable feelings towards the officer. *Was it really wrong to lie to him?* After all, she was extremely involved with someone else.

In reality, she allowed these distressing thoughts to bother her more than she needed to; ultimately, the next time Steve Spyder would ever touch her with those strong yet gentle hands, or look at her with those soft blue eyes, she would be dead.

XXXXX

As they pulled up to Vivian's work, Janice noticed that Sharon's car was still in the same spot. Maybe she was wrong. It could have been a genuine visitor. They parked, and Janice escorted Viv into the building. "I just have to pick up some papers I left here," Vivian stated. "It won't be too long".

"Hey, you two. What are you doing here?" came an unexpected voice out of the dark warehouse entrance.

"Joshua, what are you still doing here? You actually work as much as I do?" asked Vivian sarcastically.

"Hey, I got things to take care of, too, you know." Joshua walked towards his office, picked up his coat off of his desk chair, and headed towards the front door. "See you guys tomorrow," came his faint voice as he walked out of the building and towards his car.

"I wonder whose car that is out front," Janice inquired to Vivian.

"Who knows? Maybe one of the truckers got a second job to pay for it!"

They both laughed, but Janice couldn't brush off the feeling that something was just wrong with the whole scene. The whole picture was off. Joshua was hardly ever there after hours, which was around 2:00 or 3:00 pm max. It was almost 10:00 pm at the time. "Oh, well," she mumbled, "he *is* the owner. He has a right to be here just as much, or more so in reality, as you do. It just seems strange." The headache started to pry its way into Janice's head again. Suddenly the room had a red tint to it. The walls looked as if someone had painted a vibrant new color on them. A soft, neutral sound filled her ears, silencing any genuine noise around her. The walls seemed to be moving closer in towards her, along with the glass door behind her that resuscitated her exit to this strange new encounter.

Suddenly Janice looked over at her friend. Vivian had a strange look on her face; almost as if she just had a realization that seemed to be sinking in. As Janice regained focus, the walls began to recede. "What's up, Viv? You got something on your mind?"

"No . . . Let me just get my stuff and we'll be out of here." Vivian walked through the back doors towards the warehouse. Janice looked around the room to her left. There were no colors, no headaches; just a large room and a wide hall containing cubicles. She looked to her right. Only the two offices, doors shut, and an empty building were there. The walls were back to their beige color, the exit door behind her.

Chapter

Thursday Morning

Janice needed to use up the last pictures in her roll of film before she could bring it to Lori, her independent-photography partner and developer. Janice felt that the photo shoot went well. Hopefully the paper would buy her pictures again so she could start on a new look. They always bought them. She was sure they would always use her quality photos of every story, but until the check was in her hand, she didn't rely on the money. She would just use up the last pictures at Vivian's worksite. *Who knows, maybe they would come in handy for the paper someday, or just look good in an album,* she thought to herself.

As she pulled up to a parking spot at Vivian's work on Thursday morning, Janice noticed that the black viper was still sitting in the same spot it had been the day before. Sharon must have just left it at Joshua's work throughout her whole trip. Well, it would be removed that night after they had dinner with her in a few more hours. Janice got out of her car and went into the "HeadLine Goods" building where she worked. Funny, Vivian's car wasn't anywhere to be seen. Janice took a few random pictures of the workers' offices, people walking around, desks . . . *Good, the roll is finished and rewinding,* she thought. *Now I just needed to wait for Vivian to get to her desk and . . .*

"Hi Janice, you looking for Vivian?" came Joshua's familiar voice from behind her.

"Yea, where's she hiding?"

"She's coming in late today—overslept. Called about nine-ish before I even noticed she wasn't here," he said with a light laugh.

"Wow, Viv not here promptly at seven o'clock am? There's one for the books!" Janice exclaimed in a smothered wave of over-dramatization. "Let her know I stopped by when she gets in, O.K?"

"Sure, see you tonight"

"Oh, so you'll be joining us for dinner at eight?"

"No, just dropping Sharon off. Her car's still here, so I'm assuming a call will be coming in soon requesting Schaefer service from her hotel." As Joshua spoke in a seemingly light-hearted way, Janice felt that he seemed almost distant, as if he was trying to hide some deep-rooted fear. It didn't seem to fit his outward attempt at being carefree. A purple color appeared to protrude from his entire body. Janice realized she was staring and promptly looked away. "K, see you later." She waved as she left and headed back home.

Chapter

Thursday Afternoon

As a young boy, Joshua Surf had been very quiet. His parents rarely held him, and he seemed to prefer watching and observing others as opposed to talking and gaining adolescent attention from them. He would listen to his parents quarrel over menial things and wonder why grown-ups cared so much about simple material possessions rather than each other. Nevertheless, he became trained to appreciate all forms of royalties from his wealthy upbringing as he matured. Being stockbrokers and personal investors, his parents taught him that money was to be saved, appreciated, and expanded upon through various stocks and bonds, rather than spent on meager things such as candy and the like that his friends seemed to gather. Josh was taught to assemble and read such periodicals as the "Wall Street Journal" rather than collections of comic books, as the other kids his age were acquiring (unless, of course they were to appreciate greatly in value and not be read nor touched). As Joshua matured into young adulthood, he had come to the conclusion that money was the one thing that would get him ahead in life, and that people were simply to be tolerated and humored. Although at times Joshua felt misunderstood, he wanted people to know that he enjoyed them. Unknown to them, however, they were also a part of Joshua's need. He needed people. Without people, there would be no one to manipulate, and therefore, no one to conform to his every desire. Inside Joshua's mind had always been a vast extension of outreaching knowledge; knowledge that others could only imagine. He felt within himself a deep insight into his own future. It was a dark understanding of what the future might become if only he would play his cards right. And he would. Of that he was positive, and no one would ever stand in his way.

When Joshua was only a young man of eighteen years, he inherited a crucial amount of money from his parents. They passed away in a car accident while driving home from one of their regularly scheduled conferences at the firm. The car was completely totaled, as it had been driven off the edge of a small cliff. Although their bodies had never been retrieved from the burning mess, his parents had been declared legally dead within a week of the misfortune. Because he had turned eighteen less than a month before the untimely incident, he was legally an adult. He was able to collect his full inheritance along with his parents' large life insurance bestowment without any guardian-ship attached. He immediately pursued his dream of becoming an extremely successful entrepreneur and opened his own business. His company became the "in between man," buying imperishable goods from their makers and selling them to top-notch companies for well over the original buying price; thus, "HeadLine Goods" was born. The company became a huge success in only three years. By the time Joshua was twenty-one, he was completely debt-free and making more of a profit per month than people twice his age made per year. While his peers were out celebrating their age with partying at dance clubs and filling their insignificant brains with alcohol and drugs, Joshua was on his way to quickly becoming a self-made millionaire. Whatever he desired, he obtained. *And it must only continue to facilitate in the future.*

"Yes, you can meet me here at work" Joshua concluded as he spoke on his company phone. "I have a meeting to attend af-ter work today, so I'll meet you here . . . say six o'clock? Good. Yes. See you then." He pushed a button on his phone and look-ing up, asked, "Do you have those reports? This is Thursday, you know."

Vivian walked into Joshua's office with her broad smile.

"Right here." She laid the pile of papers in front of him on his desk. "Your sister, I presume?"

"Yes . . . and as I recall, you've volunteered to take her to dinner tonight while I have that meeting around eight?" Joshua asked with his charismatic smile.

"Of course. Never forget a date." As she arranged the paperwork on his desk, Vivian noticed a sheet of paper with a number scribbled on it and the name "Elizabeth" under the number. "Who's Elizabeth? Some secret girlfriend I should know about?" she mockingly asked.

"None that you should know about," Joshua flirtatiously answered. On a more serious note, he said "Just a client I need to meet with." He discarded the paper into his top desk drawer.

Vivian, practically glowing, continued to smile and ask, "Anything else you need?"

"Well, maybe a little love . . ." Joshua gave her an endearing wink. "But business before pleasures."

"So you say." Vivian turned and persuasively strolled back toward her office in the warehouse.

Chapter 7

Thursday Night

Sharon Surf loved Joshua. One could almost state that her life revolved around him. She wanted him to succeed in life, even more than she longed for her own success. She believed that he was intelligent, sharp, witty, handsome, a real "people person," and she loved to help him in any way she could. She would do whatever he would ask of her. She would tend to his paperwork, make phone calls for him, organize his warehouse, and tell people what she was supposed to tell them, according to Joshua. She would do all of this for him without even asking any questions or wanting money; after all, one day she would be a full fifty-fifty partner with him at HeadLine Goods. Most of the time she couldn't understand why he would have her tell various people different things that certainly weren't true. But she knew in her heart that Joshua was doing it all for the good of the company and not to hurt anyone; if anything, he would only spare others' feelings. That's the kind of man he was. She could only begin to understand the hurt he'd been through. She was five years younger than Joshua, making her barely a teenager when that terrible accident happened, bestowing on the family over six million dollars of inheritance. One third of the money went to Joshua, he being the eldest of the three children. The other two thirds went to his sisters, who were too young at the time to wisely invest (or spend) that kind of money; thus leaving Joshua with the full inheritance to look over. *He was so wise to hold it back from them, to not let them know; to start and control his company in order to expand and grow.* His abundance now quadrupled its amount in profit. Joshua was a wise man and deserved the love she owed to him.

As Sharon's cab pulled up to HeadLine Goods, she gathered her purse and made sure that she had left nothing in the car. "That's it on the left. Just pull into that parking lot." The cab driver slowly pulled into the small parking area outside the large, square brick loft.

"But ma'am, it be empty. No lights are here." The concerned cab driver inquired, "You want me to leave you at this place?" *Ma'am,* she thought. *The kind driver who spoke hardly any English just called me ma'am.* The last time she was referred to as ma'am was when that tall officer had called her that. *Steve. Should I tell Joshua about him? What would he think of me? Was it owed to him to know how I felt? After all, it was only harmless flirting and maybe a little feeling of . . . what? Enchantment? Was that so wrong?* She began to feel foolish about her juvenile thoughts.

"Yes, I'm fine. My brother is meeting me here." *Why does he ask me to constantly lie to everyone,* Sharon thought as she handed the driver a generous tip and walked toward the front door. As she reached for the door, she noticed that the light was on in the back. She pulled at the door and found that it was open. *Strange . . . Joshua must be at the shop already.* But it was only five thirty. He wasn't supposed to meet her until six o'clock! *What a pleasant surprise.* Sharon was extremely excited in anticipation of seeing Josh. She rushed inside. "Hello . . . anyone here?" She locked the door behind her, as it should have been. She knew that the spare key was outside under the rock, so there was no need for Joshua to keep the doors unlocked; especially since it got so dark and deserted by that time of night.

There was not a sound. Sharon walked inside and opened Joshua's office door. Startled by the dark image against the closed blinds of the window, she jumped back. "Josh? Is that you? Why are you standing in the dark?" As she reached for the light switch, a voice, almost a whisper, echoed, "Don't turn on the light".

Sharon was astonished at hearing the faint yet familiar voice. "What are you doing? What do you want from me?"

The voice echoed back to her in barely a whisper. "Do you want him? Was it worth it? The lies, the deceit . . . didn't you think I'd find out? What then? Who else will you hurt? Who else will you deceive?" The figure's arm outstretched, holding a perceptible object pointed toward Sharon. The voice not only persisted but grew louder. "I can't believe you thought you could fool everyone. I AM NO FOOL!"

Anxiety embodied Sharon as she desperately pleaded, "No, put the gun down, please. We can talk. You're not a fool. I'll tell you everythi . . ." Sharon felt darkness embed in her. The room around her shrunk slowly inward, the face of her killer standing over her in tears. Sharon uttered her last breath: "I understand."

XXXXX

They decided to at least order appetizers after sitting there over a half hour waiting for either Joshua's or Sharon's car to pull into the parking lot. Luckily Janice and Vivian had gotten to the restaurant early. At 7:45 pm, they'd been able to find a window seat with a clear view of the parking lot outside of Sharon's favorite Italian restaurant. *At least she could have been on time!* Janice thought. "How about we give her until nine o'clock. If she doesn't show, we bail." Janice looked tired, weak, and impatient. "She was supposed to meet us at eight. I think an hour is enough."

"Well, I'm hungry! I've had a very busy day. I say we order at nine if she's not here."

"Don't you have Joshua's cell number? Can you call him and see if he knows where she is?"

"Fine." Vivian pulled out her company phone and dialed the number. "No answer. Machine. You want me to leave a message?"

"No. Let's just order at nine. Maybe he'll call." Janice took a sip of her wine and looked around the restaurant. "Pretty place. Very classy."

Vivian seemed to be observing her friend. "Janice, you don't look so great. You ok?"

"Not really," a quiet reply transpired. "Somewhere late this afternoon, I got a really bad headache. Couldn't even stand up. Everything got black around me, and I felt like the walls were closing in." She sipped more at her wine. "It was just really weird. It went on for almost an hour, and then I felt this sense of . . . I don't know. *Loss.*" Janice looked uneasy, but continued sipping at her wine.

"What time was that?" Vivian felt concern for her friend.

"I don't know . . . around five . . . maybe six or so. Just like an hour before you picked me up to come here"

"And you haven't even said anything?"

"It's not like I've never gotten these . . . *feelings* before. It's no big deal. It was just more intense this time, that's all."

"I still think you should see a doctor"

"Like what, a psychiatrist? But you've known that for years!" Janice let a chuckle slip out in spite of her uneasy instincts. "Come on, let's get some food. She's never gonna show."

Chapter

Friday Morning

Janice stopped by Vivian's work again in the morning on her way to the studio. The morning pictures at HeadLine Goods were becoming a habit whenever Janice needed to use up the film she was working on in order to develop her pictures. She knew she was allowed to just waste the end of the roll, but she never liked doing that; besides, she figured she could always use bright, early shots of the morning light, whether the pictures were taken inside or out.

"Hi Janice," a kind voice came from behind her. "Ms. Shlimon isn't in yet; she doesn't get in until seven or so."

Janice turned to face the pleasant stock-boy. "Thanks, Lenny, I just wanted to use up this role of film." She snapped a final picture, and the film began to rewind, "It's on my way and all. Could you just tell her I'll call her later?"

"Sure," Lenny answered, "See ya." He retreated through the back door and into the warehouse. Janice tucked her camera in the case and headed back out the front door towards her car.

XXXXX

Lenny Johnson was a quiet worker. He opened the boxes, labeled the items, and stocked them neatly on the aisles in which they belonged. Nobody seemed to notice Lenny as he walked through the aisles doing his job; they just continued their conversations around him as he proceeded to pretend not to hear them. The peculiar thing about quiet Lenny was that he probably knew more about the goings-on of everyone there even more than they knew themselves. Lenny adored Vivian. He would watch her at her desk taking phone calls and entering different data items into her desk computer. He would always notice when she would do or change her hair, even though she looked just as beautiful when she just stuck it up in a ponytail. She was such a considerate manager; the kind of boss that workers didn't worry if she was around or not because she would never reprimand them for taking a smoke break or stepping outside. She would never punish people as long as they got what they were supposed to do at work completed.

Lenny had grown up in a loving household. His father was a private detective, and his mother was a homemaker. He was born in the northern countryside of New York, and his parents would have remained living in New York for the rest of their lives if his dad had his way. His father, traveling as a P.I. did, would visit him often, and they'd have long talks about everything and nothing. His father would have preferred Lenny become more of a "professional" in his career choice, but Lenny was happy doing what he did, so his father consented. He got paid very well, and he worked an early shift, 6:00 am–2:00 pm, which gave him, as he felt, the entire day off. He enjoyed getting off work at a time when the sun was still shining. He could look at the view of the lake behind his house with the rich green grass for miles beyond. When the sun would begin to set, Lenny would often watch the colors that it would illuminate, and he'd sit in awe for a few minutes. After darkness emerged, he would go inside to his weight room and work out for approximately forty-five minutes a night. Lenny would then get something to eat and go to bed, with visions of Vivian dancing in his head. He would dream that she felt the same way about him; that she would hold him and look deeply into his eyes. Inside he knew that if he followed through with his fantasy, he might have his dream crushed, so he decided that he would not have the courage to try to find out. Not yet. Not tonight. Tonight he would just dream of her instead.

As he stocked the new items that came in that Friday morning, Lenny glanced over at Vivian's desk. There she was, right on time. Seven o'clock. She hung her coat on the back of her chair and laid a stack of papers on her desk. *She's absolutely beautiful.* She looked up and around the counter. "Lenny? Is that you?"

"Yes, Ms. Shlimon. Today's shipment arrived already, so I just started stocking the products. Slip list is on your desk." Lenny walked towards her, adjusting his belt. "You weren't in, so I signed for it. Hope that's ok."

"Of course, Lenny, thank you." Vivian looked around. "Have you seen Joshua? Is he here yet?"

"Um, no . . . I don't know. His office door's closed. Didn't try to open it. Not my place."

"That's fine, Lenny, I'll check in a while. I just need to get some papers from him." She looked at Lenny with a tender smile. She knew he liked her. He was a very rough-looking handsome man, and she often wondered if she should just go for it and ask him out. She decided against that idea. Lenny had a very nicely built body, but other than the intense attraction she felt toward him, she didn't think they'd have anything in common. He was, well, a stock boy, and she was an executive. *It just wouldn't work.* "How many times have I told you, Lenny, call me Vivian. Enough with the formalities."

"He sure is lucky to have you working for him, Ms. . . . uh, Vivian. You do a great job."

Maybe physical attraction could be enough . . ."Lenny, would you do me a favor and just knock on Joshua's door and see if he's got the stocking papers for me?" Inquiring with a flirtatious grin, Vivian flipped her eyelashes at him.

"Sure, anything for you." He reiterated the gesture with a wink.

XXXXX

Although the phone lines constantly rang, Vivian seemed to block out the sound when she was at her desk. She just happened to glance down and notice the flashing red light on her phone.

"Hello?" she asked as she picked up the receiver and pushed the red button.

33

"Miss Shlimon?" the voice on the other end of the receiver affirmed.

"Yes . . . who's calling, please?" Vivian hesitantly asked.

"This is Officer Rose. You contacted us earlier in the week via e-mail"

"No, no I never contacted the police. There must be some mistake"

The voice on the other end seemed to alleviate some. "No, dear, not the police. You had contacted our company in hopes of finding your birth parents? Find-U Corporation. Do you re-call?"

An immortal feeling of joy and hope instantly rushed through Vivian. She felt as if she could suddenly fly if she felt the need to do so. "Oh, yes. Yes, of course. I'm so sorry. It's been a busy morning and. . . ."

"No need to apologize, dear," the kind voice over the phone reiterated. "I just wanted to let you know that our company is looking into your situation as we speak. We've found that your birth parents were in fact from the Chicago-land area." Officer Rose hesitantly cleared her throat. "We would like to meet with you sometime in the near future in order to discuss this farther if you could give us a few minutes of your . . ."

"What do you mean *were* from?" Vivian cautiously inter-rupted, a minor feeling of desolation coming over her. "You said *were,* not are. Is something wrong? Are they . . ."

"Please, please, dear. If we could just have a few minutes of your time, I'd be happy to meet with you and let you know everything, but not over the phone. Yours is a very strange case, and—"

Vivian cut the kind officer off in mid sentence. "Let me get your number." She picked up a pen and tore a piece of computer paper off her desk. "OK, I'm ready . . . what is it? Yea, six-three-oh, uh huh, four-nine-eight-three, got it." She repeated the number back into the receiver. "Strange case, huh?" Vivian felt an overwhelming anguish come across her, heavier than it was the first time. Just as she was about to ask the kind lady what would be a good time to meet, a frightful shriek disarrayed her. Startled, she jumped from her desk and dropped the phone. Loud voices and sobs protruded from the front of the building. Vivian immediately ran towards the cries and pulled open the door to the adjoining front-end of the building. All she could see was Joshua's office door open and practically everyone who was employed at HeadLine Goods standing around and peering in. Her heart sank.

XXXXX

"Elk Grove Police, Steve Spyder"

The voice on the other end of the phone was frantic. Steve sat up and motioned to his partner to come over. "Right on it, we're leaving now." He hung up the phone. As usual, Friday was the beginning of the weekend-crime. Up until now, Steve had had a pretty quiet day. "Bret, we need to get over to Head-Line Goods. There's a problem."

"Yea? What kind of problem?" Bret inquired.

"Some stock-boy found a stiff in one of the offices." Steve grabbed his jacket, and they both headed out the door and towards the car.

XXXXX

Lenny put his left arm around Vivian, and his right hand on her cheek. "I don't think you want to see this, Ms. . . . mm, Vivian. It's not a pretty sight." He tried to lead her back to her office, but she resisted. Laying her hand on his, she looked into his deep brown eyes and softly began to ask the feared question. "Lenny, is it? Is it Joshua?"

"No, Vivian, he's not in there. I saw him outside just after I found . . . you know, not him." Lenny hesitated and felt completely unhinged, yet still held Vivian with a firm, strong grip close to his body. "The police will be here any minute. You need to go back to your office." His voice increasing in sound, he looked towards Joshua's office. "Everyone needs to go back where they belong! The police will handle this!"

XXXXX

Standing over the corpse, Steve felt an imperishable darkness absorb throughout his entire body. "This is vile"

"What, you act like you know her?" Bret Mirza asked his partner.

Steve leaned over and gently placed his strong hand on her face for the last time. "Yea, I met her in the airport earlier this week. She just flew in. The day of the fuel crash, remember? We blocked the exits for a while at the airport."

"This is your goddess?" Bret asked, stunned. He felt that his partner would never get over this one. Steve hadn't stopped talking about the wonder woman he'd met last Wednesday, and now that Bret finally got to meet her, she was dead. Bret knew that there was no way Steve would let this case go unsolved. Whoever committed this heinous crime against Sharon would pay his dues for it. That was for sure. "Sharon, right?"

"Yea."

"Did she say what she was here for?"

"Yea, to visit some friends and her brother," Steve despondently replied.

"Well, let's start with him. He work here?"

"How should I know?" Steve tenderly placed his sturdy fingers over Sharon's astonishing eyes and delicately closed the lids. Together, anger aside anguish emerged inside the officer. "Such a waste. We're gonna get this guy, Bret." Steve turned and exited the office as the paramedics ran from their ambulance outside and towards the building's front door.

Chapter

Friday Afternoon

"Oh, Vivian, I came right over. I just heard the news on the radio!" Janice wrapped her arms around her friend. "Is it really Sharon? How's Joshua? Is he here? Does he know?"

Vivian hugged Janice back, "Yea, it's Sharon. She's dead" She leaned on her desk and picked up a pen. "Lenny saw Joshua just after he found Sharon . . . Shot. I'm sure Joshua knows by now."

Janice sat down next to Vivian. "Are you ok?" She asked.

"Sure. I didn't even like her, but there was a minute there that I thought it was . . ." Vivian drifted off, looking down and circling a number with her pen on a torn sheet of paper.

"Joshua?" Janice asked.

"Yea," Vivian replied. "'Find-U' called today. I think they found my birth parents."

Janice suddenly felt a little hope arise inside of her. "Yea?"

"Well, it also sounds like they might be dead," Vivian mournfully stated. "How come everything has to happen all at once?"

Janice reached out and held Vivian's hand. Silence between friends can be the most soothing kind; the kind that cures the ailments of the heart. Suddenly the silence was broken with the sound of the door opening. A deep voice, gentle yet rough at the same time, emerged.

"Which one of you is Vivian Shlimon?" Steve asked as he looked toward the two women. Suddenly, his eyes met Janice's, and he felt a fervent sensation that he'd only felt once before in his lifetime; ironically, it was only that last Wednesday that he'd felt such an attraction toward someone. Two in one week; what were the odds? Curiously, this attraction, though just as powerful, was still distinct from the one he had felt upon looking at Sharon. Janice had a dark lure, a mysterious air surrounding her. She had deep, penetrating eyes, and long, lustrous auburn hair that almost glowed in the warehouse light. Her skin was pale yet supple. She was fit yet tender, and he longed to hold her—to protect her.

Looking up at the cop, Vivian stated, "That's me. I'm Vivian."

Steve snapped out of his visionary hero role and became aware of his surroundings once again. "I need to ask you a few questions." He pointed at Janice and said, "You too, Miss . . . I didn't catch your name?"

"That's because I didn't give it." Smiling, Janice held out her right arm. "Janice. Pleased to meet you officer . . . ?"

"Steve."

"Officer Steve?"

"No. Just Steve." He should have answered "Spyder," but his mind wasn't in full focus. Two in one week was just too much for him to handle.

XXXXX

"But I saw you right after I found her." Lenny persisted on stating the facts to Joshua.

Joshua could not understand the importance of the issue. "Lenny, you need to just forget that I was even here. I don't want the police questioning me about any of this. I want to stay out of it."

Lenny looked disturbed. "I'm not gonna lie"

"I'm not asking you to lie. I'm simply asking you not to point anything out if they don't ask." Joshua was growing more impatient with the obtuse stock-boy, whom he now regretted hiring three years prior. "Besides, you're the one who found her, not me!"

Lenny looked around cautiously. Upon realizing that they were alone, he reinstated his concentration on Joshua. "I know she's not your sister."

Joshua met Lenny's eyes. *No need for panic, this dense stock-boy can't hurt me.*

"What are you talking about?"

Lenny smirked at Joshua. "You thought I was just a dumb worker. You never even noticed when I was there while you and her were kissing. I ain't got no sisters, Josh, but if I did, I sure do know I'd never kiss them the way you've been kissing Ms. Surf."

Joshua glared at Lenny. *No need for alarm. He's just a stupid stock-boy. He isn't capable of doing any harm.* "Why won't you just do what I say? Why do you persist on agitating me? Nobody questions me!"

"Funny, Mr. Surf, I thought I just did. Now what are you trying to hide from the police?" Lenny stood strong. Standing next to Joshua, Lenny looked very intimidating. If he did feel intimidated, Joshua never let it show.

"What do you want?" Joshua sternly asked.

"Well, first I want to know what's going on around here," Lenny openly replied.

"Only first?"

"Yea, then when I hear your side of the story, I'll decide what I want in return for my silence, or even if I'll keep silent." Lenny turned with a mocking smile on his face and walked toward the door. "I'll be in touch, Mr. Surf, you can count on that"

Joshua felt a repulsive amount of anger rising inside of him. That impudent, overpaid stock-boy! How dare he threaten someone of Joshua's position! Joshua Surf needed to get rid of Lenny. *He's no good to the company. Lenny. Stupid stock boy!* Joshua thought, *he thinks he is smarter than me, the owner? He thinks he can just walk up to someone with class and demand his will? Doesn't he know that I get whatever I want?* The anger rose inside of him. *Nobody will stop me. Nobody even tries. I am higher than all others. I get what I want when I want it!*

Lenny will be disposed of. He is nobody. He will aggravate me no more, and I will see to it myself.

XXXXX

Janice felt a little uncomfortable in the presence of such a magnificent man. She tried to concentrate on anything else, but his masculine hands and strong figure kept drawing her eyes back to him. "Well, I figure it must have been Thursday night, around five or six o'clock in the evening. That's when I just, well, I felt odd."

Although Steve was incredibly attracted to this woman, he didn't trust her. She was too intense. There was something about her that almost frightened him. "We'll let the autopsy handle that for now. As far as we know, it could have been Friday morning." He watched her intensely. There was no reaction. She just gazed back into his captivating eyes.

"Maybe it was just a feeling, but I guess we'll find out soon enough." She smiled. He obviously captivated her. "If that's all, I need to get back. Vivian's really shaken up about this" She stood up and faced the back door. "Will you be here for a while?" she asked, still not facing Steve.

"For a while. Until we either find the gun or give up trying." Steve felt hopelessly nervous in the company of Janice. He felt like he could either take over the world or crawl under it to hide. She definitely had a hold on him. "I'll see you around then?" he asked with anticipation.

"Sure, I'm usually here." Without turning to face him, she proceeded through the doors and on to Vivian's turf.

XXXXX

Bret worked his way toward Steve. "I don't think it's here," he stated discouragingly. "I think we've talked to everyone except the owner."

"Is he here?" Steve asked

Bret pulled out a notepad and fingered through it. "No, wasn't even in today."

Steve looked around. "Was he here last night?"

"Why? You got a lead?" Bret looked up from his notepad.

"Something else doesn't add up. The guy who found the body, Lenny, he never said he saw . . ." He flipped through his notepad. " . . . Joshua Surf."

Steve, puzzled, looked at his partner. "Was he supposed to have seen him?"

"According to your young lady friends—Vivian in particular—the guy who found the body saw Joshua immediately after." Bret shrewdly smiled at Steve. "At least the one you've got your eye on isn't involved."

Steve desolately responded, "I wouldn't be too sure of that yet. We need to find that gun."

XXXXX

As Vivian put away all her office possessions, she picked up the torn sheet of paper. A phone number was written on it. She sat at her desk and quickly scribbled the name "Rose" on the top of the paper, then added "Find-U."

"What's that?" Janice asked as she looked at the torn paper.

Vivian looked up at her friend. "It's that place, you know, where I can find my birth parents." She looked down at the paper. "I guess I didn't set a time to meet with them. Sharon and all happened right as I was talking to some lady. Rose."

Janice stood up. "Well, you'd better make your appointment or you'll just be going on insight alone." Smiling, she put her hand on Vivian's shoulder. "And you know where that can get you." *Nowhere.*

Viv looked up and smiled with Janice. "I have a date tonight." Her smile widened.

"With who?" Janice was shocked.

Vivian musically replied, "Somebody hot," with a broad smile.

"Are you for real?"

"Yes ma'am. I finally just decided to do it. He asked me, and I said yes."

"Are you going to keep me in suspense forever? Who?"

Vivian twirled around and snatched up her purse. "Lenny," she replied.

"Good for you!" Surprising herself, Janice felt an overwhelming feeling of relief prevail over her. She gladly accepted that her best friend did not have a date with the strong, stunning cop whom she herself so admired.

XXXXX

"Yes, officer, she stayed here every few weeks. Joshua Surf arranged her visits and a taxi to pick her up at the airport." Kyle was genuinely confused. *Why were these cops asking so much about Sharon?* "What's going on?" *Maybe,* he thought, *they found out what I had already discovered. I'd better not offer any information until I talk to her. She's a great lady. I don't want to do anything that might incriminate or hurt her. I'll ask her tonight when she retires to her condo.* "Is she ok?"

"We're just trying to figure out why she was here and who she was associating with during her visit," Bret bluntly responded. "You work here full-time?"

Kyle looked irritated. "Could you just please tell me what's going on? She hasn't checked out yet. Her plane doesn't leave until seven tonight."

Steve Spyder laid a hand on Kyle's shoulder. "Kyle, were you close to Ms. Surf?"

"No, she was my friend. I mean, I only knew her when she stayed here, but after more than a year . . ." Kyle looked at the sympathetic way the officer was looking at him. He realized the physical gestures were not standard for Chicago officers looking into someone's false identity. "Why are you asking me about Sharon?" Kyle sternly asked, brushing Steve's hand off his shoulder.

Steve stepped back from the wide desk. He looked at Bret, then back at the petite man with the baffled expression standing behind the desk. "Sharon's been murdered, Kyle. It happened sometime between three and seven Thursday night."

Kyle felt dizzy. He sat down on the chair behind him. "What do you . . . are you sure it was . . . but she was so. . . ." Disorientation filled his head, and he just stared at the floor in bewilderment. "No. This can't be happening."

Steve looked at his partner and motioned to him. "Well, if you remember anything that might help us, anything at all, please don't hesitate to call." He handed Kyle a card, which

42

was incoherently taken from his hand. With words eluding him, Steve turned and walked out the door as Bret followed. Once outside the hotel lobby, they walked towards their car. "Definitely not our guy, but he knows something," Steve observed.

Bret agreed but knew that the doorman was too stunned to talk just yet. "He'll call. You can bet on it."

Chapter  10

Friday Evening

Lenny was more excited than he had been in years. He was skipping his nightly regime that particular Friday in order to accommodate someone he had loved for years. As he lit the tall candles setting on either side of the small dinner table, he hummed to himself. He had finally worked up the nerve to ask out his beloved Vivian. True, he took advantage of a moment when she was filled with utter vulnerability and despair, but she complied nonetheless. He picked up a bouquet of flowers that he had purchased on his way home from his encounter with Joshua. As he laid the flowers between the candles, he admired his work.

He felt inspired, encouraged, and stimulated. He should have asked her out months ago. He didn't know if it was the fact that Vivian might feel something for him, or if he was still pumped up from his dealings with Joshua Surf earlier that day, but Lenny felt good about himself—*powerful*. It was a feeling that he hadn't experienced in his life before, and he started to understand what his father had been talking about all those years. *Status,* he thought . . . *Rank* . . . *Position.* At that moment, although it was recognized knowledge only between him and Joshua, Lenny was at a higher status than Mr. Surf, and he liked that feeling. *Power.*

The phone rang. "Hello?" Lenny asked as he picked up the receiver and brought it to his ear.

"Lenny? It's Vivian," answered the voice on the other end.

Lenny felt crushed. *I knew that she was going to cancel her date with me. I should have picked her up,* he thought. *What kind of man asks a delicate flower like her out on a first date and makes her come to him? What kind of idiot doesn't show her that he cares enough for her to go and pick her up . . . bring her back to his place?*

"Yes, Vivian, how are you? Are you still coming over? "Lenny timidly inquired.

Vivian giggled on the other end of the receiver. "Yes, of course I am. I'm just running late. I should be there in about a half-hour. Is that ok?"

"Sure, no problem," Lenny replied. A feeling of relief emerged over him. He suddenly was experiencing further suppressed feelings that he hadn't considered before. He wanted her to know that he *was* somebody—that he wasn't just a stock boy. He wanted Vivian to look up at him and think highly of him. *Status. Rank. Position.* He knew things. He wanted her to understand that.

XXXXX

Janice skimmed through the pictures that she had taken Friday morning at Vivian's work. There was the office door where the horrible event had taken place the night before; at least that's what the medical examiner had concluded. Between three and seven Thursday night, someone had heinously murdered Sharon Surf. There in Janice's hands were pictures of the morning after, before the body was discovered.

These pictures aren't going to help anything, she thought. There's the closed door with the undiscovered body lying behind it. She looked closer at the picture, focusing on the window next to the office door where Sharon's body resided. The window was facing the street behind Headline Goods. There he was, clear as the morning sky. Joshua Surf outside on the grass. It appeared to Janice that he was getting ready to get into his car, keys in hand, but there was no car to get into; at least not one within the view of the window.

How odd, she thought, that he blatantly denied being at the office at all on Friday before the police had contacted him about his sister. *What would he be hiding? Why would he not admit he was there? The murder didn't even happen that day. Why would he need to lie?*

Janice picked up the phone and dialed the number on the card in her hand. "Yes, could I speak to officer Spyder, please?" she asked, a small grin forming on the sides of her mouth. She needed an excuse to see him again, and it appeared she had one. "Oh, he's not? No, no, it's not an emergency, but it is of some relevance to a case he's working on. Could you just have him call me when he gets in tomorrow?" She felt herself blush; she proceeded to give them her number. "Yes, that's my number. No, my *personal* number. Thank you." Smiling, she hung up the phone and decided to call it a day. *I'd better get some sleep,* she contemplated as a pleasant chill ran down her spine. *Tomorrow I'll be spending a lot of quality time with Officer Steve Spyder.*

XXXXX

Vivian was enchanted by Lenny's apartment. Although it was small, it was decorated incredibly. There was no clutter lying around, and it had just enough quality decorations on the wall to give the place a look of elegance and touch of class. The colors were rich yet subtly laid, and the aura of his home was sweet and welcoming. Lenny handed Vivian a glass filled with a rich chardonnay. "I'm so sorry I didn't even offer to pick you up. I was just thinking of making dinner and all, and I forgot my manners."

Vivian gently took the glass of wine from Lenny's strong hands. "That's fine. I don't mind driving. Next time you can pick me up." She smiled her broad smile, whch sent Lenny's whole body into a feeling of utter weakness.

"So there'll be a next time?" Lenny smiled and looked deep into his goddess' eyes. "You really are an angel, you know."

She responded to his stare, laid her glass of wine on the table, and moved closer to him. A feeling of nervousness over-

47

whelmed him, and anxiety seemed to flow throughout his entire body. He felt stiff. He couldn't move. Was his untouchable beauty actually coming on to him? Sweat began to protrude from his back, and suddenly he was self-conscious of his panic.

Vivian couldn't see this side of him, he thought. She couldn't know that he had such a weakness. Thoughts raced through his mind at an alarming speed; he couldn't keep up with them all. She gently moved in closer, placing her hand on his wine glass. She removed it from his grip, aligning the glass next to hers on the table. His mind went blank. All he could see was his dream coming true in front of him. He placed his hands on her waist and drew her to him. They kissed passionately for minutes. He slowly rubbed his hands about her, wrapping his arms around her and cupping her delicate head in his sturdy hands.

I love her, he realized. *I love her with an intensity that just can't be ordinary in this world.* He wanted to be with her forever, in that moment. *All I've ever wanted my entire life is right here, right now.* He could only pray to God that he meant as much to her as she did to him.

XXXXX

"Simmons. S-I-M-M-O-N-S. Simmons. Yes. Elizabeth. Yes, I'll hold." Joshua felt agitated and irritable. He'd been on the phone for over an hour trying to contact someone in Texas who knew his girlfriend. Soon the police would figure it all out. *Lenny,* he contemplated, *stupid stock boy. Threatening me. ME, Joshua Surf. Who does he think he is?*

"Yes, hello? No, I understand. I'll try again during your working hours. Thank you anyway." Josh hung up the phone. *Keep yourself calm, stay cool,* he thought to himself. "Ridiculous business hours." He got up, walked towards the bar area in his living room, and poured himself a drink. It was whisky, no ice.

What do I do now? He wondered, *who else knows about Sharon?* Lenny. *Curse him.*

Joshua downed the shot he was holding. He paced back and forth, agitating himself further. He returned to the bar and poured himself another. He looked around his house; everything was expensive, quality. He worked hard for this, all of what he had acquired; his position, his possessions, his life. No one should take that away from him. *Especially not a stupid, soon to be obsolete stock boy.*

XXXXX

What felt like just seconds but was in reality was over ten minutes later, Vivian and Lenny parted lips. He looked down at her wanting eyes. "Vivian, I . . ." She put her finger to his lips.

"Don't speak, Lenny. I want this more than I've ever wanted anything. I need you right now."

Lenny looked down at the floor, still holding her around the waist with both his hands locked firmly on each of her sides. She admired his strong build as her arms were around his neck; *his strong, obviously athletic, neck.* "What is it Lenny? Did I come on too strong for you?"

He looked up at her batting eyes. "Vivian, you've been through a lot tonight. I know you're vulnerable."

"Isn't that why you invited me to your house, Lenny?" she replied flirtatiously.

Lenny was startled by the insinuation. *How could she think that of me,* he wondered. *Doesn't she know how much I've loved her over the years?* Still holding her, he stared past her eyes towards the window. *Of course not; how could she know? I've never even hinted to her the deep love that I've felt for so long.* It was time for a serious talk. "Sit down, Vivian, I'll get our dinner. We need to get something cleared up."

Chapter 11

Saturday Morning

"Morning, Steve," Bret said with a mocking smile on his face. "Coffee?" he asked as he held out the cup to his partner.

"What do you know?" Steve questioned. "You want to share it with me, or are you gonna just sit there with that dense smile on your face all day?"

"You got a message last night after you left. Your girlfriend wants you to go see her this morning." Bret comically waved the note-slip in the air.

Steve sat up, grabbing the paper from Bret's hand. "Gimme that you jackass." He looked at the note. Smiling, he turned to the phone and picked up the receiver.

"Gonna go gawk?" Bret asked, sipping at his coffee.

Grinning at Bret, Steve stated, "At least I have someone to gawk over".

XXXXX

Lenny woke up to the bright sunlight peering through his window. He was almost surprised to find Vivian lying in his arms. It wasn't a dream; she had stayed the night. They had had a wonderful dinner and talked about so much, sharing their feelings, hopes, and dreams. It had gotten so late by the time they had finished eating and talking that they decided she should stay the night. He had offered her the spare room, but he was more than happy to just hold her close. All his dreams were coming true, *and she cared for him.* Wow; this goddess cared for *him.* He was on top of the world.

"Lenny? Are you awake?" came her delicate voice from his side. He looked over and down at her, smiling, treasuring the moment forever. "Good morning, my love," he stated as he leaned in to kiss her.

Vivian pushed away, embarrassed and still smiling. "Oh, Lenny, I have morning breath. Let me use your bathroom." She got up and retreated to his facilities. *Still beautiful,* he thought, *even first thing in the morning.*

XXXXX

Before he could leave to meet Janice, Steve's extension began to ring.

"Spyder," he stated as he held the phone to his ear.

"Yes, this is Tammy Evette, from the hospital," came the reply on the line.

"Yea, you're the medical examiner. What can I do for you?"

"Well, there's been some confusion here, and I was wondering if you could come down to the hospital and have a look at what we've found."

Steve sat upright in his chair, flexing the muscles in his back. "Why, what's going on?"

"It seems that the lady who died . . ."

"Sharon Surf," Steve bluntly replied.

"Well, it seems that she matches the identity of an Elizabeth Simmons from Houston, Texas. She even has all her identity on her person, right down to her social security card. We looked her up and sure enough, that's who we have here. I don't know why she was posing as. . . ."

The lady on the other end of the receiver seemed to be talking somewhere into the distance. Writing down the information he'd acquired, Steve interrupted, "Ms. Evette, could I come down there later on today and take a look at those identifications?"

"Sure, Officer, just come in whenever it's good for you. I'll be here."

Steve hung up the phone. Baffled, he looked across the room at Bret. His partner met his eyes and knew something was amiss. Walking towards Steve, Bret inquired, "What's going on? Who was that?"

Steve spun the notebook around for Bret to read.

Bret took a look at what Steve had just written and said in a comical tone, "Wow. So this means she sure ain't Josh's sister, huh?" Bret, smiling, looked up at Steve. He then halted his smile when he saw the despair on his partner's face. "I guess we need to re-question Mr. Surf."

Chapter 12

Saturday Afternoon

"Lenny, you've already done enough. You don't have to make me breakfast," Vivian said as she flirted with her new-found love. "I shouldn't even be here."

Lenny smiled at her as he flipped the eggs in the pan. "It's more like lunch." He grinned at her and winked. "Anyway, I like cooking for you. I like you being here." He walked over to the freshly brewed coffee and poured some into two cups. "Coffee?"

"Sure." Vivian preferred tea, but Lenny was so kind, she figured she'd take the coffee.

He looked at her. She was stunning, *and here. Here with me.* Could life get any better?

"Cream or sugar?"

"Yes please."

"Both?"

"Uh-huh." She smiled happily. Lenny was so nice. She wished he wasn't just a stock boy. *I wonder why he never strove to be more.* He walked over to her and handed her the cup of coffee, cream, and sugar. "Here you go."

She carefully took the cup from his hand and sipped at the drink. "Thank you, Lenny."

"I like the way you say my name."

"Why, do I say it wrong?"

"No, I just like hearing it coming from your mouth." He touched her chin with his right hand and gently brought her face towards his. He leaned over and lightly kissed her lips. She returned the kiss with a light blush.

"Oh, Lenny, where have you been all my life?"

"Right in front of you, I guess it just took a murder to bring us together"

They grinned at each other, both feeling a little embarrassed for finding such happiness through another's pain.

XXXXX

Janice got up to answer the door. She had been watching one of her favorite sitcoms on the television. As she opened her front door, there he stood; the object of her desire. "Hi, Officer Spyder. I was expecting you hours ago." she said with a kind smile.

"Yea, well, something came up."

"About the case?" she asked, still grinning. He couldn't help but smile back at her. She was a lovely sight to behold; so mysterious, so stunning.

"Yea, about the case . . . You said you had something for me?" He blushed at the thought.

Janice turned and walked back towards her computer desk. "Yes, pictures. Come on in." She glanced back towards the door. "Your partner's welcome in, too."

"Thanks." Bret followed Steve into her house. It was a very bright house. It had light yellow paint and one entire wall made of glass. There was a striking view of a small lake just outside.

"Nice place you got here," Steve said as he looked around. "You live alone?"

"No, Vivian's my roommate. You met her at Headline Goods, remember?" She handed Steve the pictures. He took them from her and started to flip through them.

"You say these were taken on Friday morning?" He passed the pictures over to Bret.

"Yea, I had a role of film to use up, so I just took a bunch of pictures at Viv's work before going to the studio."

Steve looked accusingly at Janice. "Friday morning, the day after the murder. You just happened to take pictures?"

"Well, you don't have to take my word for it. The date's printed right there on the bottom!" Janice didn't like where Steve was heading with his looks and actions. "Why would I lie about that?"

"You're a photographer, aren't you?" Steve looked her in the eyes. *Wow, she's a knockout.* He realized that he needed to get past the affection he felt for her if he was to do this right.

Janice answered him. "Yes, I take the pictures and my partner develops them."

"What's your partner's name?"

"Lori."

"She live here too?"

"No."

"Where's she live?"

"Not here, why?"

"Why won't you tell me?"

"What's it to you?"

"More than you need to know."

"I'm trying to help you here!" Janice snatched the pictures out of Steve's hands. "What's your problem?"

"I'm not the one who's got a problem, lady."

"Well, I would beg to differ!"

"Oh, yea?"

"Yea."

Bret walked between the two ardent bickerers. "OK you two, cool it. This isn't a competition." He nudged his partner away from Janice with one arm and held his other arm between them. Looking at Janice, he put his hand upright. "Do you mind if we keep these pictures for a while?" he pleasantly asked her. "We do need to get going, but it would really be of help if you wouldn't mind. We do appreciate your assistance on this case."

"Your partner here coulda fooled me on that one." Janice handed the pictures over to Bret.

Bret took the pictures, gave Steve a foul look, and turned back towards Janice. "Thank you for your cooperation. We'll be in touch." Looking at Steve, he mumbled, "Come on, Romeo."

Both officers turned and walked out the door. Just outside, Steve turned and looked back at Janice. "Hey, Janice."

"What, Officer?" she callously replied.

"Call me Steve." He gave her one of those darn endearing smiles of his.

She couldn't help but let out a little grin. "Yea, well you can call me 'Miss. Cloud.'" She turned and closed the door. Leaning with her back to the door, she felt anxious, upset, and just a little blissful. She realized that she was even more attracted to that officer than she had been before he arrived. *How could I be? He practically called me a suspect!* She couldn't believe she still wanted to help him, or see him. *But I do want to be near him, very much even.* As she stepped away from the door and looked out the window at the two cops, she suddenly realized that she didn't even get a chance to show them what she had discovered in her pictures. "Oh, well, *he's* so bright, let *him* figure it out. Not my problem anymore," she muttered as she retreated to her couch.

XXXXX

"We're glad you decided to call us, Kyle. Just relax and tell us what you know."

Kyle felt awkward being at the police station, but he wanted to help Sharon as best he could. After thinking about it, he decided that the only ethical thing to do would be to go to the police and tell them what he had discovered during her stays at the hotel.

"Well, yea, he wasn't her brother. He just made sure she told everyone in Illinois that he was."

"How do you know this?" Bret asked the benevolent man.

"She used to cry sometimes at night. After we'd gotten to know each other, she'd sit and tell me stuff about her life."

Steve perked up. "Yea?" he quizzically asked.

Kyle looked over at the other officer. "No, no, nothing like that. She was a real nice person. She just needed a shoulder to cry on." He brightened up a little. "I used to be a bartender, you know."

"Great," Bret replied. "Go on."

"Well, you know, they were lovers. Her real name was Elizabeth. She lived in Texas and was going to be moving out here so they could get married. He promised to introduce her to his *real* sister and his family and all after she moved. She thought he was great. She felt sorry for him, seeing as how his parents died when he was a kid."

"Yea, died a month after he turned eighteen; just old enough to inherit the whole scha-bam," Bret spat out sarcastically.

Steve asked, "So he *does* have sisters? Are they around?"

Kyle repositioned in his seat. "Yea, well, he's got one sister named Sharon for real, and another one whose name he doesn't know."

"He doesn't know his own sister's name?"

"Yea, well, he put her up for adoption when his parents died. Sharon, or . . . um . . . Elizabeth says it's because he was just a kid himself and couldn't raise both his sisters alone. She said he signed the ok for the adoptive parents to change her name."

Bret looked the boy in the eyes. "What do you think, Kyle?"

Kyle met Bret's gaze. "I think the guy's a creep. I wouldn't put it past that scum to do this to poor Elizabeth."

XXXXX

"Lenny, have you ever thought about moving up in the company?" Vivian timidly asked. "I don't mean that your job now isn't, well, sufficient, it's just, you know . . ."

Lenny looked at her with disappointment on his face; *she wants to change me.* "I like my job."

"I know you do, but don't you want to be more than just a stock guy?" As soon as she said it, she wished she could take it back. "I don't want to hurt your feelings, Lenny"

"Well, you just did." He turned away from her. "Besides, my job's a lot more than you think."

Vivian walked over to him and put her hand on his shoulder. "I know, you're right."

Lenny felt an anger building up inside him. *Here she is, the only girl I've ever given my heart to, giving me sarcasm,* he thought hopelessly. He wanted her to know that he was smart. *I know things that others don't.* He wanted her to realize that his was a very perceptive job. "Don't mock me, Vivian."

"I'm not mocking you, really. I just wondered if you ever

thought about it." She removed her hand from his shoulder. "That's all, just wondering."

Lenny turned to face her. "Don't you want me for who I am?"

"Of course I do." She leaned over and kissed him on the cheek.

"Vivian, I know things that go on at HeadLine, more than most people know."

She looked at him awkwardly. *What's he talking about,* she wondered uneasily. "Like what, Lenny?"

Lenny looked her straight in the eyes. "I know who killed Ms. Surf."

XXXXX

Joshua wondered if it would be too much of a risk. After all, it wasn't even two full days after Elizabeth had been brutally killed. Was it too soon to dispose of that dimwitted stock boy? The daylight was leering into night darkness. It was Saturday night; a perfect time to catch Lenny off guard. As he loaded his gun, he made sure the safety was on. He definitely didn't want anything accidentally being blown off in his pants. His door buzzed. Startled, he walked over to the speaker. He wasn't expecting anyone. He pushed the intercom's speak button. "Yes?"

"Joshua Surf? This is the police. We just have a few questions regarding Sharon Surf, if you have a minute," the voice over the intercom stated.

Josh pushed the speak button again. "Hold on." He retreated to his cabinet, where he gently placed the loaded pistol. Returning to the front door, he buzzed the officers up.

Chapter 13

Saturday Evening

Vivian was astonished. "Lenny, how can you know? Did you go to the police?"

Lenny shifted his stance. "Well, not for sure I don't, but I think I do."

"Did you go to the police?" Vivian persisted.

"No."

Vivian was horrified. "You can't just go around accusing people of something this critical! Someone could get in a lot of trouble for something they didn't do. Don't you see that?"

Lenny suddenly felt dense and inadequate. "Yea, but I *do* know stuff, and I figured I could tell *you,* Vivian, even if it's just a suspicion."

She suddenly felt foolish for going off on Lenny the way she did, and that endearing smile of his just made her melt. "I'm sorry, Lenny. Yes, you can tell me anything. Really." She put her hand on his cheek and smiled. "But for now, just tell me the facts. Only the things that you know, without a reasonable doubt, are true."

Lenny sat down and shifted in his seat. "Well, I do know that Ms. Surf sure as heck ain't Mr. Surf's sister. I don't know who she is, but I know he's cheating on his girlfriend with her and calling her his sister."

Vivian felt a fuming infuriation beginning to grow inside

her stomach. "What do you mean his *girlfriend?* He has a *girl-friend?*"

Lenny continued, still looking down at the ground. "Well, like I said, I know he's got a sister named Sharon Surf, and another sister that ain't related to him no more somewhere out there."

Vivian started to feel irritated. "Lenny, look at me." Lenny looked up at her, she asked in a calm and steady voice, "What did you mean by his *girlfriend?*"

Lenny suddenly realized that Vivian was furious under the cool mask she wore. "Vivian, you don't still have feelings for Mr. Surf, do you? I mean, after last night, and today, and us?"

She composed herself, trying to suppress her mounting anger. *How could Lenny know how I feel about Joshua?* "What do you mean? I never had—"

Lenny cut her off in mid sentence. "Yes you do. I'm telling you, sweetheart, I know everything that goes on at that company. No one even notices that I'm there when they tell all their dirty little secrets."

Vivian felt foolish and childlike trying to hide her feelings for Joshua. "Lenny, I'm sorry. You're right. We have something special that I'd like to build on. Josh is part of my past."

Lenny smiled at his goddess. "We'll work on that, ok?"

"Tell me about his girlfriend anyway, just for fun?" She batted her eyes at him in that flirtatious manner that got her practically everything she had ever wanted in life.

"Well, I know he talks an awful lot to someone named Elizabeth. He tells her they're gonna get married, and how someday everyone will know."

Elizabeth, she remembered, *he told me that she was a client.* "This makes you think he killed Sharon?"

Lenny looked into her eyes and said matter-of-factly, "Well, sure. Don't you think so?"

"But why?"

"'Cause the girl that goes by Sharon Surf threatened to tell Elizabeth about them."

"You know that?"

"Well, no, I was just assuming. But, you know, that's the way I figure it."

Vivian stood up and paced the room. "Well, if Sharon isn't

his sister, where is she? You say he really does have a sister named Sharon?"

"Yea. And another one that was only six when his parents died."

"How old was Sharon?"

"She's four years under him, which would have made her fourteen at the time."

"Any other family?"

"None that I'd ever heard of, and believe me, Vivian, I'd heard it all" Lenny felt revived. Here was Vivian, his love and the foremost big shot in the company under Joshua Surf, asking *him* for information. He knew that someday he could prove to her that he was important.

Vivian turned and met his gaze. "Where are these sisters? Why hasn't he ever even talked about them?"

Lenny laughed a little. "He has mentioned at least one of them. He even introduced us to her; except it wasn't her, was it?" Lenny let out a chuckle under his breath. "Just turned out to be one big lie, is all."

XXXXX

Joshua felt imposed upon in his own home. "Look, it's getting late. I've already told you all I know."

Officer Spyder smiled a shrewd smile at the corporate executive "No, Mr. Surf, I don't believe you have. See right there in the picture? That sure looks a lot like you, doesn't it?"

Joshua looked at the picture with his image just outside the window. The date and time were on the bottom right corner. "You know, any developer can just change the time or date on his own film"

"Not so sure about that, Josh. What I am sure of is that's you standing right where you claimed not to be last Friday." Bret knew they had their man.

Steve stepped in. "So, Josh, you want to tell me something I don't know, like why you lied to us about being at the scene of the crime?"

Joshua stood up abruptly. "That was not the scene of the crime! Elizabeth died Thursday night. I read the report. I wasn't anywhere near her that night!"

"You just made two grave mistakes, Josh. We have witnesses who've told us that you had plans to meet her at the location where she was killed at 6:00 Thursday night. That would put you at the scene of the crime, now, wouldn't it?"

Joshua pointed his finger at the officer. "Now, wait. Yes, I was *supposed* to meet her there at six, but when I got there, she had left a note on the door. I have it." Joshua moved around his living room clumsily, trying to find this note as he fumbled through desk drawers.

Bret leaned over to his partner. "What's the other mistake he just made?" he asked, smirking.

Steve looked at the fumbling idiot and then back at Bret. "He called her 'Elizabeth,' not 'Sharon.'" They both smiled as Joshua shuffled back towards them. He held a crumpled note with tape folded over the top. Bret took the note, unfolded it, and read it out loud: "Sorry for the inconvenience, but I had some official business to take care of. Thanks anyway." On the outside of the note was the word "JOSH" written in all caps with a red marker. Bret thought it was strange that the note was written in plain blue ink, and Josh's name was written with a marker. The bottom of the note was torn off. Bret looked up and asked, "Where's the rest of the note?"

Joshua looked stunned. "What do you mean the 'rest'?"

Bret held the note between his first two fingers, waving it at the executive. "The rest of the note. The part you tore off."

"I didn't tear any off. I swear. That's how I found it taped to the front door of the building when I got there at six. Her car was gone. I figured she'd left."

Steve intervened "What did you say? Her car?"

"Yea," Josh replied, looking back at Steve. "Her car was there all week, even when she wasn't. When I found the note Thursday night, her car was finally gone from the visitor's spot." He looked confused yet irritated. "I didn't kill her. I loved her; well, at least I think I did. I was going to marry her! That's something, isn't it? Why would I kill her?"

"You were going to marry your sister?" Steve recapped.

Josh looked hopeless. "She wasn't my sister."

Bret was beginning to feel less and less sure that they had the right man. "Why did you lie to us, then? Why did you tell us you weren't there Friday morning?"

Joshua realized that there was no use trying to hide his secret. "Because I didn't want anyone to know who she was."

Chapter 14

Sunday Morning

Vivian wasn't sure she should be bothering Ms. Rose on a Sunday. The nice social worker had left her home number on Vivian's answering machine the day before, and she'd been reluctant to call her back. She felt bad leaving Lenny the way she did, full of questions. She almost felt like she had spent the last few hours with him interrogating the poor guy. He didn't seem to mind her asking so much though; *in fact,* she thought, *he seemed to enjoy it after a while.* She would call him later.

She picked up the phone and dialed the number written next to it.

"Hello?" a caring voice sounded over the line.

Vivian quietly asked, "Is this Sara Rose?"

"Yes it is. Who's speaking?"

"This is Vivian. Vivian Shlimon from—"

"Yes, yes, of course, dear," Sara interrupted. "I'd left you a message. I was hoping you'd call. How wonderful."

"You said you had some good news for me?"

"Yes. I suspect you know there's both good and bad news, but when I had talked to you on Friday, I'm afraid I only had the bad part. Now there have been some discoveries that I think you'd be happy to find."

Vivian felt that hint of hope start to open up inside her. "Really?" She sat upright in her chair and picked up a pen.

"Yes. When would be a good time to meet with you, dear?"

"Well, I could do tomorrow. Any time, really. Our work's been kind of . . . temporarily shut down 'cause of the crime scene and all."

"Oh, yes, I heard all about that on the news. Was she a friend of yours?" The concerned woman over the other end of the receiver genuinely seemed to care about others. *It's nice,* Vivian thought, *to have such people in the world.*

"Not really. I didn't even like her, to be honest." Vivian let out a muffled laugh. "So, is tomorrow ok?"

Sara Rose hesitated, and then answered, "Yes, that's fine. What time's good for you, dear?"

"Whenever."

"How about noon? We could do lunch."

"Fine with me. Where do you want to meet?"

"How about that lovely little Mexican restaurant right by your house? You know, the one next to the grocery store?"

"I know it too well," Vivian happily responded.

"Great. I'll see you at noon then."

Vivian felt good. She picked up the phone to tell Lenny her exciting news.

XXXXX

Lenny had aggravated Joshua for the last time. Josh couldn't believe how naïve he'd been. He had thought that the police were just doing their job and questioning him as they would anyone else. Lenny must have told them. *That's why they went in search of evidence to link me with the scene of the crime,* Joshua thought. *They had already been told that I was there; told by that intrusive stock boy.*

The police wouldn't be back on a Sunday. *I have to act quickly before Lenny tells them anything else he might know about.* Joshua went to the drawer he had left the gun in the night before when the cops had so rudely interrupted him from disposing of evidence. He opened the drawer and picked up the pistol. He held it in his hand as though it was precious. He could feel that if he just disposed of that good for nothing laborer, all his worries would vanish.

Joshua placed the gun in his pocket, put on his shoes and coat, and headed out the door.

XXXXX

The phone was ringing. Lenny jumped out of the shower, wrapped a towel around his waist, and rushed to answer it. Could his sweet Vivian be calling him so soon? He smiled at the thought. "Hello?"

"Lenny?"

It was her on the other end. He was overwhelmed with a sense of passion. "Yes, Vivian, you must miss me."

"Of course, Lenny, but I was so excited, I had to tell someone"

"Excited about what?"

"I have a meeting with that lady I told you about. Remember? From Find-U Corp?"

"Yea, I thought you weren't going to meet with her."

"She says she has good news now."

"No more bad news only?"

"Well, still the bad, but topped by good now." Vivian giggled at the sound of what she just said. "You know what I mean".

Lenny felt happy for her. "Good for you. When you meeting her?"

"Noon tomorrow."

"Well, then, that makes you free tonight?"

Vivian flirtatiously answered, "Well, actually, I have plans"

Lenny frowned. "With who?"

"You, silly."

Lenny brightened up immediately. "Great. This time I'll pick you up; say around six?"

"Why so late?"

"If we get off to a late start, maybe you'll have to stay the night again." Lenny couldn't help but feel his face flush.

Vivian was delighted. "I'll see you at six, then."

Chapter 15

Sunday Afternoon

Bret was feeling more and more helpless. "So what about the car, Steve? No one's said anything about a car being parked there all week."

Steve looked at his partner. "Maybe no one said anything because nobody thought it was relevant."

Bret put his hand on his head, rubbing lightly. "So, what now? We go looking for this car? This Viper? You think the guy who did Sharon in took the car?"

"Elizabeth."

"What?" Bret looked up

Steve put his hand on the papers in front of them. "Her name's Elizabeth."

"She's dead, Steve."

"You don't think I know that?" Steve felt like he was being ridiculed. "What about the note? The handwriting expert says it's a dead ringer for hers."

"Yea, but what if she wrote it to someone else?" Bret inquired. "Someone who tore off the last half and made it look like that's all there is to the note?"

"You think Joshua Surf has the other half?"

Bret looked down at his hands and regrettably stated, "No. There's something going on with him, but I think he was telling the truth. I thought he was our man."

"Might still be," Steve responded.

Steve and Bret had to find the other half of the note and the black Viper. "Where you want to start?" asked Steve.

"How 'bout your girlfriend? She seems to know more than she's letting on."

Steve looked inquiringly at Bret. "You noticed that too?"

They both headed outside the police station and toward their police car.

XXXXX

Joshua felt influential, vigorous. He had parked his car blocks away from Lenny's house and walked the rest of the way. He felt an empowering feeling; he planned to shoot Lenny in broad daylight. He was in the back of Lenny's house looking into a window. Luckily, the whole yard was enclosed by a fence. No one would see him, he contemplated. He would stick the silencer on his gun, walk in through the unlocked back door, shoot Lenny in the head, and leave. *No one cared about this common laborer,* he thought to himself. *Nobody would ever even find the body until well into the middle of the week when he fails to show up to work several days in a row.*

Through the window, Joshua could see Lenny coming out of the bathroom with wet hair. He was freshly clothed. *Perhaps I should make it look like an accident,* Josh thought. *I could make it look like the dimwitted idiot slipped in the shower and killed himself. The police are already agitating everyone with too many questions; maybe an accident would be the more intelligent move.*

Joshua slipped the silencer onto his gun, anyway; just in case. He slid the gun back into his jacket and looked around the yard for something strong enough to hit Lenny with that would do him in.

XXXXX

Opening her front door, Janice felt excitement and resentment all at once. "Hello, officers. I wasn't expecting you today."

Steve walked into her house when she opened the door.

"Yea, well, you were expecting us early yesterday, so this balances out." Bret followed Steve inside.

"Won't you come in?" Janice asked sarcastically as the two men brushed past her.

Steve looked around the room, then down into her beautiful brown eyes. There was a small, affectionate smirk on his face. "Thanks, don't mind if I do."

Bret intervened, "What can you tell us about a black Viper parked outside your work?"

Janice looked stunned. "It belongs to Sharon Surf. She left it there while she was in town. Josh just drove her or got her a taxi while she was here. Why?"

"What about Friday morning after the murder?"

"I guess it wasn't there. That's weird. It was her car." Baffled, Janice looked towards the officers. "Whoever killed her Thursday night must have taken it. Did the medical examiner say her keys were on her?"

Steve put his hands out in front of him, palms facing Janice's inquiring mind. "Whoa, slow down there. As I recall, we ask the questions; you answer them."

Bret turned towards his partner. "Hey, Steve, she's just trying to help."

Just as Steve was about to state his thoughts on the matter, Janice suddenly dropped to the floor. Steve rushed to her aid. Reaching for her, he frantically inquired, "You ok? What happened?"

Janice, sitting on the floor, placed her hand on her head. *Everything's black. The room keeps spinning.* "It's just like Thursday night," she said, eyes still closed. "Just like when Sharon was killed. I felt it. Someone else just died."

Bret, alarmed, looked at his partner as he helped Janice up and to the sofa. Steve felt anxiety run throughout his body. A deep fear ran up his spine and within his bones. It was fear that he couldn't do anything to help this delicate lady in time. He gently placed his arms around her and lifted her. Laying her on the sofa, he said, "Are you ok? What happened?"

Wrapping her left hand around the officer's masculine neck, Janice placed her right hand on her forehead. "I just know," she softly stated.

"What do you mean?" Steve inquired. "You knew when Sharon was killed?"

Eyes still closed, sitting upright on the couch, Janice helplessly responded, "Somebody just died! Go help them!"

Chapter  16

Sunday Evening

Looking down at the brainless stock boy who laid there helpless, Joshua smiled. *That wasn't so hard after all,* he thought. Blood drenched the back of Lenny's irrecoverable head.

"How 'bout now, Lenny?" Josh said out loud. "What are you going to do now?" Josh strolled around the dead body. He laughed to himself as he thought of strong, stupid Lenny trying to blackmail him; giving away his secrets; telling the police about Sharon. "You can't hurt me now, stock boy." Josh started to giggle to himself. "You really thought you could outsmart me. *Me,* Joshua Surf." Watching Lenny's unresponsive body, anger and anxiety started to build within Josh as his voice grew louder and louder.

"Well, what's your plan now, Lenny? You have a plan? You want my money now?" Josh turned towards the motionless body. "Or maybe you want my job?" Joshua felt pure hatred toward Lenny as the notion of blackmail empowered his thoughts.

"Answer me!" Kicking the still body, he felt the anger grow into rage. "Why didn't you just keep your fat nose out of my business?" Kicking Lenny's lifeless body once more, Joshua threw the candlestick at the corpse.

"I should have taken care of you years ago."

Upon realizing that his voice might have carried through

the open windows, Joshua suddenly calmed himself. Coming back to reality, he realized that he had to dispose of the corpse in a fashion that would lead the authorities to believe the idiot had done it to himself.

I have to move fast, Joshua thought. *I have to move this body into the tub and then clean up any evidence that he died here in the kitchen.* He picked up the candlestick that ultimately brought Lenny's life to an end and placed it in the sink.

Just calm down and make sure everything's done right, he thought. *After all, I have the rest of the day to clean up this mess.*

XXXXX

Steve placed his left hand behind Janice's head, lowering her onto the couch. He gently positioned his right hand onto her flushed cheek. Looking closely into her eyes, he softly stroked her face.

"Are you ok?"

She looked up into his concerned blue eyes. Speechless, she tried to say that she just felt these things sometimes; that she didn't know how or why it happens to her. She wanted to help, but as she looked into Steve's sky-blue eyes, she couldn't seem to get out any words, much less the right ones. His face was so close to hers. His hands so gently embraced her that if she didn't know the situation, she would believe that they were in a passionate embrace. She let an affectionate smile come out and decided against clearing her mind.

Steve did not look away; instead, he wondered, *should I let my lips meet hers now or simply continue to hold her, to caress her?* The thought of looking away from those stunning brown eyes never passed through his mind. He liked this embrace, and he intended to stay in it as long as possible. By the look she was giving him, she didn't object.

Somewhere in the distance, Bret cleared his throat. Steve reluctantly broke himself free of his instincts. Still holding Janice in the same manner, he turned to face his partner.

"You want to go check on that?" Steve requested.

"Check on what?" Bret sarcastically asked.

Steve grinned at his partner. "Someone dying."

Rolling his eyes, Bret turned and headed toward the door. "I'll let myself out, thanks."

XXXXX

The adoption agency was very eager to assist in the official police work. When Bret called them on Saturday, a compliant lady told him that he could come by anytime Sunday, and she'd be happy to help. Since his partner was taking the evening off, or so Bret would assume, he decided to check out the Surf family history on Sunday evening. He was actually surprised that anyone would be working, but when he called, the lady on the other end of the line was more than accommodating.

As he pulled up to the building and into the almost-empty parking lot, Bret noticed the appealing view surrounding the structure. It was the time of year when the trees were just beginning to loose their leaves, and the colors of the earth were magnificent. The lake next to the land was rippling lightly to the sway of the wind, as were the trees. The air was crisp and clear as the sun began to set, surrounding the entire scene with a rich flow of colors from the sky. He could understand why people felt hope as they entered this building.

He let himself inside the unlocked door and walked up to the desk, where a smiling receptionist awaited him.

"Hi. I'm Officer Sanders. I spoke to a lady named Pam on the phone earlier."

"Yes, just a minute, please." The receptionist pushed some buttons and picked up a phone. Glancing back up at Bret, she smiled again. "She'll be with you in just a moment." Motioning towards the waiting room, she added, "You can have a seat if you'd like."

"Thanks." Bret helped himself to some water and sat down to wait.

XXXXX

Steve felt helplessly vulnerable leaning over this incredibly attractive woman. He couldn't hold back his anticipation any longer. He leaned into her, using his hands to cup her head and embrace her face in order to pull her closer, allowing their lips to meet in a passionate embrace. She responded to his desire by wrapping both her arms around him and keeping him close.

They eagerly kissed for well over a minute when Janice's phone began to ring. She ignored the sound until the answering machine picked up. She then heard Vivian's depressed voice. "Hi, Janice. I guess my affair with Lenny was just that; an affair. A brief affair . . . ," assumed the disheartened voice on the answering machine.

Janice looked towards her phone, interrupting her and Steve's intense embrace. Apologetically, she whispered, "Steve, I need to get that."

Steve softly lifted his hands. Janice turned, shifted to a sitting position, and picked up the phone. "Viv? What's the matter?"

"He said he'd pick me up at six. It's almost seven now. I've been here at work waiting for him for almost an hour ,and he didn't even call."

Steve stood up and helped himself into the kitchen. *Just my luck,* he thought. Taking a Diet Pepsi out of the refrigerator, he turned to face Janice through the doorway opening. "Is everything ok?" he asked her.

There was a pause on the other end of the phone. "Who was that, Janice?" Vivian inquired.

Janice directed her answer to Steve. "Yea." Then she again spoke into the phone "No one. What's up?"

"No, I heard a man's voice."

"Really, it's not important. What did you say? Are you ok?"

Vivian sighed over the phone. "I think I came on too strong. I invited myself on a date with him."

"Did you try to call him?"

"No. I'm not going to bother him. He should be calling me."

"Something could have happened to him."

"Yea," Vivian desolately responded. "He could have come to his senses and blown me off. Just like every other guy . . . no one ever sticks around!"

Janice let out a sigh of discontent. "I'm serious, Viv, he could be hurt."

"Not likely."

"Do you want to come home?" Janice asked.

Steve sat down next to Janice on the sofa. He gently placed his left hand on hers. She looked at his soft blue eyes as a small grin emerged from her lips.

"No, I'll leave you alone with your invisible man." Vivian let out a small laugh. "I'll call you when I leave here tonight, but I'm going to stick around a while & get some files logged."

"OK, don't worry about Lenny. I'm sure it'll all work out." Janice hung up the phone. A wave of guilt began to rise inside of her, and she looked back toward Steve. He sat looking at her, sipping his drink.

"Somebody's hurt?" he asked Janice.

"Lenny just blew off his date with Vivian."

"I'll ask him about it tomorrow when I see him."

Janice looked surprised. "You need to talk to him again?"

"Wouldn't hurt. Now tell me about this hallucination of yours."

Stunned, Janice turned to face Steve directly. "It wasn't a hallucination! I just . . . I don't know . . . I felt something."

"Like what, a phantom?"

"More like an apparition." She felt herself tensing up. "Are you making fun of me?"

Steve set his can of soda on the table and took both of her hands in his. "No, no. Really, I just don't know what to think of all this voodoo-hoodoo stuff." He looked into her eyes with that charming, bewildering look that made her want to just forgive anything he could possibly do wrong. He sighed and slowly said, "I've just never heard of someone 'knowing' when someone else dies . . . what is it, a vision?" He shifted nervously in his chair. "A feeling? What? Are you like that psychic guy from the Dead Zone?"

Janice looked away from him and thought for a few seconds. "No. I don't know." She looked back up and met his eyes again. "If I don't even know, how am I supposed to tell you what it is? And why would you even believe me?"

"Maybe I don't. I just want to." He smiled, placed his hands on her cheeks, and leaned in to kiss her again. She angled away from him slightly. "I don't know if we should be doing this," she stated, a questioning look on her face.

"Neither do I," he answered as their lips met once again.

XXXXX

"Mr. Sanders, I presume?" Stretching out a hand in front of her, she said, "I'm Pam. Pam Lily. Pleasure's all mine."

Bret set his plastic cup on the table and stood up. Reaching for the lady's outstretched hand, he introduced himself. "Hi. Call me Bret."

"Now, Bret, what can I do for you?" the courteous lady happily asked.

"I talked to you earlier. About the Surf history, you recall?"

"Oh, yes indeed." Straightening out her flowery, button-down shirt, the large, giddy lady looked around the waiting room towards her desk. "Yes, yes, now where did I put those papers?"

Bret couldn't help but smile at the frivolous manner of the woman. He recalled the sense of lightheartedness as he entered the building. He couldn't stop thinking about how the feeling continued to reside as he came inside, as well. "You have the adoption information?"

"Oh, yes. We keep very credible records here." Smiling, Pam shuffled over to a desk behind the reception counter and practically disappeared under a pile of papers. "Here it is," a happy voice announced. A hand holding a large manila envelope emerged from behind the stack of papers, followed by Pam's jolly face. "I had these all put into one load for you, Officer Bret," she stated as she opened the envelope and reached into it. Bret looked intensely as she pulled out a page and skimmed it over. "Yes, right here in black and white. You see this?" she asked, shifting in his direction. She was still looking at the paper but now pointing at it with her other hand that encompassed the envelope. Bret leaned toward her and read over the page.

"This is an address in Chicago, right off 57th street." Bret looked at Pam. "This is current. He still owns this house?"

"Apparently so. Never sold it, never even tried to rent it, but the bills have been kept up, and it's in his name."

Bret moved his gaze down the page. "There *is* a Sharon Surf?"

"Yes, and another one—see here? She was given up for adoption when she was only six years old." Looking up at the officer, Pam's face contorted. "Do you think he even knows about her?"

Bret met the woman's gaze. "I would put money on it. Could I get a copy of these?"

Pam's face perked up again. "Well, who am I to stop official police business?"

She turned and headed towards the copy machine with the envelope as Bret thanked her for her help. *If there really is a Sharon Surf,* he thought, *where is she, and who was Elizabeth? Why would she have claimed to be Joshua's sister? Wasn't she having an affair with him?* It was getting too confusing even for him.

XXXXX

Steve reluctantly answered his cell phone to hear Bret's voice on the other line. "You find out anything?" Steve asked his partner.

"Not about your phantom murder, but yes, I got some news for you. You want to meet up somewhere get some coffee?"

"Tonight?"

"You have plans, I take it?"

Steve looked over at Janice positioned next to him. Her eyes were wide with anticipation. "Yea, you could say that."

Bret could hear the exhilaration in his partner's voice over the phone. He blandly stated, "It can wait. I'll see you in the morning."

Chapter  17

Monday Morning

"Coffee has got to be the best thing mankind has ever invented." Bret let out a sigh before he took another sip of his black coffee.

Drinking his orange juice, Steve looked over at his partner. "Coffee comes from a coffee bean. Mankind didn't invent it," he stated matter of factly. "Besides, it's too early to be contemplating coffee."

"Easy for you to say. I still don't know how you can resist it." Bret had always liked the true taste of high-quality coffees. Unlike those people who hid the taste with sugars and creamers, he enjoyed every untainted delight of the coffee itself. "Well anyway, where do you want to start after we eat?"

Steve, still looking over the papers that Bret had brought that morning, started to cut some of his pancakes and took a bite. He washed them down with more orange juice. "I guess we should take a trip to 57th street, see what's there."

"What about your girlfriend's phantom murder?"

"I don't know. I say we check out facts first." Steve took another bite of his breakfast and shuffled in his seat. He looked around, bemused. "Besides, if there was some murder that took place last night, that would mean. . . ." He drifted off on his thought as Bret sarcastically intervened, "What would that mean? That your girlfriend's psychic?"

Steve snapped back to his thought. "Bret, I think we both know she's not psychic."

"Then what would you call it?"

"I'm just saying that maybe she just . . ." He put his fork down and leaned closer to his partner. "Maybe she just knows too much. You get me?"

Bret sat back and looked at Steve. "And you don't want to see it."

XXXXX

Rob Johnson was starting to get agitated by his son's lack of concern for other people's deadlines. As he pulled up to Lenny's house, he once more tried to call him on the phone. He had specifically made plans with his boy to meet him Monday morning and had waited over an hour for Lenny to arrive. No call, no show. Rob had tried to call Lenny at least a dozen times, and he wouldn't even answer his phone—neither of them. Perhaps he was with this young lady friend he spoke so prominently about all week. Was this the same girl he'd had his eye on for the last year, Rob wondered? The name sounded familiar. Vivian. *Nice name. Well,* he thought, *boys will be boys, even when they're supposed to have grown up into men.*

"Lenny, you in there?" Rob hollered as he rapped on his son's front door. There was never a spare key hidden somewhere. Those who knew him well knew that. Although the door was locked, Lenny never locked his back door. Lenny was always trusting of his environment. Many had advised him against his trusting nature over the years, but Lenny was never felt that he had to lock himself in and others out. Lucky for his father, today was no different. The back door was unlocked and welcoming. As Rob walked around the house, he felt almost as if he was intruding upon his son. *What if Lenny is in there with his lady friend?* Rob weighed the outcome and decided upon checking in on his son, despite the possible embarrassing consequences. He opened the back door and walked in. The kitchen was clean as a whistle. Lenny had always been tidy, but it looked as if he had gone to special measures to actually clean the place. *This girl of his must be something special,* thought Rob.

"Lenny? It's me, Dad. You in here?" There was nothing; not a sound. "Lenny?" He raised his voice. "I've been trying to get a hold of you all morning." Again, there was only silence. "Lenny . . ." As he turned left into the hall and came upon the scene in the bathroom, he almost fell with agony. He was hardly able to make a sound, yet he still feebly called out, "Lenny? No . . . Lenny, my Lenny . . ." His voice dwindled and he felt his knees shift. Before he knew what was happening, he was on the ground. Tears freely falling from his eyes. He felt fear, dread, anguish. He was his only son. "Oh, Lenny . . . what's happened to you? . . ."

XXXXX

"This is it, Steve. Pull over here." Bret pointed at an abandoned house in the middle of nothing. There were no other houses or any buildings close by. It was very strange for a spot in Chicago to be so abandoned.

"How do you know this is it?" Steve inquired.

"Get your head out of the clouds and look," Bret responded.

As Steve looked at the house, he noticed the driveway that went around the back. He noticed something that, until spotted, was barely enough to see. Once his eyes fixed on it, it was extremely obvious. It was the front end of a black Viper. "The car," Steve feebly said.

"You noticed." Bret was already getting out of the car and walking up the drive. He was ready to go for his gun if needed. "Back me up, Steve, and get your head back to this world. We could be in for something."

XXXXX

Vivian just couldn't understand why anything Sara Rose was asking her was relevant to the information she was to receive at noon that day. "Haunted mansion? I'm sorry, Sara, but I just don't understand why you're asking me about a—"

"I know it makes no sense, dear," Officer Rose interrupted, "but I'm just wondering if you know anything about it. Maybe you've heard something?"

"No, I haven't, why? What is it, some sort of Halloween thing?" Vivian was genuinely bewildered.

"Well, apparently, there's a house in Chicago. I was looking over the paperwork, and there's a clause in it. Unfortunately it's been abandoned—but paid for, if that makes any sense, dear."

Unfortunately, to Vivian it made no sense at all. "So someone's been paying for nothing?"

"Well, land is very expensive, dear. It's quite an equity to have. Especially in the city; you could tear down the old house, although it's probably some kind of landmark now. Maybe you could fix it up or—"

Vivian realized that the nice social worker was just speaking with her own perspective in mind, but it all just sounded like foolish babbling to her. She cut her off in mid-sentence. "Wait a minute, Ms. Rose. Hold on. Why are you telling *me* that *I* could do all this to some haunted house that I've never even seen? What's going on here?"

Sara realized she'd been going on and straightened up. "Well, I'll see you at lunch and show you all the information. You'll understand then. Noon, right?"

"Yea, sure, noon. See you then." Vivian hung up the phone. She sat there for a minute thinking about the confusing conversation she'd just experienced.

XXXXX

"There's nothing here, Steve, just the car." Bret looked around at the small field surrounding the house. There was a playground to the far right of the field and the backs of houses on the other end. The street was pretty close to the front of the house, but the driveway circled around the back and over to the other end of the old place. "Why would someone just keep the land and let the house fall apart? He coulda made a killing renting this place out."

"Not in the shape it's in now." Steve pushed the squeaking door and stepped up onto the creaky floor. Some pre-teens were running around in the field a good distance from the house, yelling and laughing. Bret followed the sounds and watched the kids as they waved and ran, then came closer and ran again.

"I'll be back, Steve," he stated as he walked in the direction of the children.

Steve watched his partner as he also inspected the house. It was bright outside. The light shined through the many windows of the house, revealing how magnificent it must have been in its time. As he walked around the house, he took note of the firm foundation and solid walls. Inside, he observed that it could be just as magnificent as the outside if it was ever to be restored. Even the furniture was left to rot with the remains of what could have been kept up. "I don't understand this guy," Steve thought aloud. "This place could be a goldmine."

"Yea, looks that way." Bret's familiar voice came from behind Steve. "These kids seem to have familiarized themselves with it over the years"

Steve turned with his hand still on the beautiful porcelain counters. "Yea?" Five pre-teen kids were gathered around Officer Bret. Steve couldn't help but smile at all the excited faces asking him and his partner questions about being a policeman.

"Is it exciting?" one of the kids inquired to Bret.

"It can be."

"Do you get to catch the bad guys?" a young girl asked Steve.

Steve smiled at her and answered, "Well, sometimes, with the help of good citizens like you kids."

The girl's eyes lit up. "Really? I can help police officers?"

"Sure you can," Bret responded. "In fact, you all can help us right now by telling us about this house."

XXXXX

Rob Johnson realized that he had to separate the fact that Lenny was dead in the tub, and the love he had for his son if he was going to keep his sanity. He had to get to a phone. *Don't touch anything,* he told himself. *This could be a possible homicide.* There was blood all over the tub. The shower wasn't even on. There was no water in the tub. *Too much blood.* There was no sign of a struggle. He just had to get to the phone and touch as little as possible. *This is definitely a crime scene.*

Chapter  18

Monday Afternoon

Vivian was a little anxious to meet with Sara Rose after their conversation earlier in the day. She sat patiently in the front of the restaurant awaiting Ms. Rose's arrival. She practically jumped up at everyone who walked in ringing that bell attached to the door. Finally Sara showed up, smiling as usual. "Hello, dear, how are you?" she cheerfully asked.

"Fine, and you?" Vivian politely responded.

"Let's get a seat, shall we?" They followed the doorman, who picked up two menus and led them to a booth.

After ordering drinks and looking over the menu, Vivian started the real conversation. "So, what about this house? You said you had good news for me?"

Sara looked up from her menu and closed it. She laid it to the side and looked into Vivian's eyes. "Well, I do realize that I wasn't making much sense earlier, dear, but I was just excited to find out even more."

"But I don't even know the first part of the even more." Vivian smiled.

"Yes, I realize that, so I'll start at the beginning." Ms. Rose took a deep breath. "You have a brother *and* a sister. I looked and looked, but I just couldn't find your sister . . . until yesterday." A wide, proud smile emerged on Sara's face.

"I don't understand; you know where my biological family is?"

"Both your sister and your brother, but of course I found him right away!" The smile expanded.

Vivian felt a rush of overwhelming excitement develop inside her. She didn't know what to say or what to ask, or even what she should be thinking. "And my parents? Did you find out anything else about them?"

Ms. Rose's smile faded and she looked a bit perplexed. "Now, dear, I would have thought your brother must have told you by now. You know they died when you were six . . ."

"What do you mean? You said you just found him." Vivian's thoughts were racing.

"Well, yes, I admit, I only just realized what was going on, but he takes care of you, doesn't he, dear? I mean, you *do* work for him."

Vivian wasn't one hundred percent positive that she knew exactly how Janice felt when she got her blackouts, but she was pretty sure that she had a good idea of what one of them felt like at that precise moment in time. The room seemed to spin around her. All the information began to feel like pounds weighted in her head. The minute pieces of the puzzle in her life began to fit together. She couldn't believe what she was beginning to realize as she heard herself feebly say, "Joshua? Josh is my brother?"

XXXXX

As they drove back to the suburbs, Steve made a call to some inspectors to check out the house on 57th Street, not to mention the car. Neither Bret nor Steve could figure what was going on with that Viper. All they knew was that Joshua Surf had something to do with all of this. He may not be their man, but he could at least lead them to whoever was.

"I don't like him," Bret concluded as Steve hung up the phone.

"Who? The kid?" Steve laughed.

"Joshua Surf."

"I know, just messin' with ya. How 'bout those kids, huh? Crazy imaginations." Steve leaned his chair back.

Bret was still thinking about Joshua and what role he had in all of this, but he responded to Steve's conversation. "I don't know, they make a bet, who's the brave one who'll go into the 'haunted house.' All kids do that sorta stuff."

"Yea, what do you make of all this?" Steve looked over at Bret, who was obviously preoccupied with something.

"Why would he just leave a house like that to rot, but still pay the taxes and not even rent the place out?"

"Don't worry; our good inspector will come up with some of those answers within a few hours."

"Or maybe Josh will give us a straight answer this time."

"Yea, good luck with that theory."

XXXXX

Joshua had just taken a long shower and decided to relax and reward himself. He had just opened a fine bottle of wine aged to perfection for his tastes when his door buzzer went off. Pressing down on the speaker, he inquired, "Who's there?"

"Joshua Surf? It's Officer Sanders again; we just have a few more questions for you."

Joshua felt the infuriation rise inside himself again as he thought, *When are those dense cops going to get off my back?* He had worked hard yesterday. He had cleaned all day and not protested. *It wasn't even my own house! It was that dimwitted stock boy's place, but had I complained? No. All I wanted was a quiet evening alone without those annoying policemen bothering me. Is that too much to ask? Apparently so.* "Come on up," he resentfully stated as he buzzed them in.

"Hey, Josh, why don't you tell us about the house you own on 57th?" Bret asked as soon as the door was opened. Walking past Joshua, who was standing in his bathrobe, both officers entered the house before Josh had the chance to decline. "It's a real beauty. Why didn't you ever keep it up? Or maybe tear it down and use the land for something productive?"

Joshua, shocked, tried to reply. "How did you know—"

Steve turned and faced Josh, cutting him off in mid-thought. "We know all about your little games, Josh. Now I think I'm looking out for your best interests when I tell you that you need to start playing straight with us." He turned his back on the scrawny man in the bathrobe and headed towards the kitchen. Opening the refrigerator, he restated Bret's question. "What's with the house?"

Joshua felt intruded upon, vulnerable, defenseless. "So I own a house in the city. Who cares? I haven't been there for years!"

Bret walked up to Josh. "Years, huh? You mind telling me what your girlfriend's car was doing there?"

Joshua was genuinely baffled. "What do you mean?"

"It's not that hard to figure out, Josh." Pointing to Joshua, Steve slowly spelled it out. "Your girlfriend's car," he motioned towards the window, "was over there at your house."

Bret intervened before Joshua could answer or defend himself. "It seems pretty simple to me, Josh. You wiped her out, used an old note that she wrote, tore off the bottom half, took her keys, and drove her car to a place you thought it'd be safe. A place that you believed her car could just rot away, along with the house."

Joshua started to defend himself before Steve once again cut him off. "But what you didn't count on was us finding out about your house and in turn, finding your girlfriend's car there."

"I didn't kill Elizabeth. I told you, I loved her. Besides, the house—I just pay the taxes." This once powerful man looked broken down. He looked like he was going to cry. He no longer looked like the high stock market player that he used to pretend to be, but more of a feeble soul waiting to perish. "The house doesn't really even belong to me. My sister owns it."

"Your sister?" Bret mockingly inquired.

"Yea, my little sister." Joshua decided to play the victim, the sufferer, the prey. He knew he could play the part and play it well. He hunched his shoulders over in a distressed fashion and quivered his chin just enough to make it look believable. "When my parents died, I was only a child." He slowly walked over to his sofa, dragging his feet slightly. "I had a little sister who was only six years of age. I couldn't take care of her; I didn't know what to do." He looked up at the officers, meeting each of their eyes, and then looked back down at his feet. He knew he had them fooled. He could see it in their eyes. *Joshua Surf is no one's fool.* He realized that he could pull off anything to perfection. "I don't know where she is now, but the house was supposed to go to her when she came of age." He once again met each of the officer's eyes. He needed to know that they were sympathizing with him; that they believed him. "It's in their will." He looked down again, knowing that he was pulling it off. Although he was playing the fool, he felt the power begin to rise within him. He had to work very hard not to smile with supremacy. "But when I grew up, I couldn't find her. I tried, but she was lost. I only paid the taxes in her memory. It's like a sanction to her." Still looking down, he waited for one of the officers to speak. *Silence. Good. They're no longer trying to ridicule me; to break me down,* he thought favorably. *They believe that they have accomplished their goal.* "I just never went back. I couldn't bear to think of our house, the house we all grew up in . . ." He let himself trail off; *more of an effect that way.* When neither of the cops spoke right away, he finished his thought as he slowly looked up to their faces. "Maybe Sharon . . . the real Sharon, not Elizabeth, brought the car there. Maybe I can still find her." He knew this would have been impossible; however, he genuinely had no idea why the car was there. He would have to look into that later. For that moment, he was just relieved that was all they were after.

Just as Steve was about to say something, his phone rang. He picked up the receiver. "Spyder here." His posture changed. He stood up straight, suddenly unaware of the pathetic man sitting near him. "Where are you now?" He motioned to Bret. "Stay put. We're on our way."

"What's up?" Bret asked his partner.

"We need to go." Facing Joshua Surf, Steve put a hand on his shoulder. "Thank you for being honest with us. We have to go. There's been an accident."

Bret turned to Joshua. Not as empathetic as his partner, he stated, "We'll be in touch."

XXXXX

With sirens on, driving the car at a high speed, Steve purposefully punched his hand on the steering wheel. "Why did she have to be right on this?" he angrily asked himself.

Bret, realizing that his partner was only talking to himself, answered him anyway. "You had no way of knowing."

"But I should have checked it out; I shouldn't have gotten involved with her if I even suspected she was a . . ."

"Murderer?" Bret finished Steve's thought.

"No, of course I don't think . . ." Steve unbelievingly trailed off his own sentence.

Bret sympathized with his partner. "Look, Steve, no one thinks that she killed anyone. She was with us when it happened." Grabbing at any bit of hope in order to assure his partner, he skeptically stated, "Maybe she really does have some sort of *insight.*"

"You believe that as much as I do," Steve answered despondently. He turned a sharp corner, sirens blaring. "But how would she have done it?"

"Hey, come on, Steve, we don't even know if she had a reason. Let's not put the cart before the horse."

Steve looked at his partner despite the rapid driving. "Whatever, man."

XXXXX

Arriving at Lenny's house, the police car almost drove into the large tree in the front of the yard. They pulled into the driveway and shut off their siren. Both of them jumped out of the vehicle and headed towards the front door. Finding the door locked, Bret knocked on it as Steve put his right hand on his gun. Inside, they could hear movement as the front door opened. An anguished man with noticeable red circles around his eyes weakly stood in the doorway, arms slung hopelessly at his side. Bret spoke first. "Are you Rob Johnson?"

The man quietly answered. All hope and care seemed to be drained from him. "Yea, Lenny's in the bathtub. I tried not to touch anything." With that statement, an abundance of tears began to stream from the man's eyes. He just stood in front of the officers and cried freely. "He was my only son. This wasn't an accident. Someone wanted it to look like an accident. This is a crime scene."

XXXXX

As the forensics crew looked around, taking pictures and

doing their job, Rob Johnson sat out on the front porch and stared into oblivion.

"Why don't I give you a ride home," Steve offered to the disheartened father of the victim. "You're not helping your son or yourself by just sitting here. The forensic scientists and the police will figure this out."

Rob just sat there with no response. Bret came over to where Steve and Rob lingered. "Steve, could I see you for a minute?" They both walked toward the driveway.

"Do you want to question the victim's girlfriend or should I?" Bret thoughtfully asked Steve. "It's Vivian Shlimon, Janice's friend." He waited for a response from his partner, though Steve just stood there silently for a moment. Bret continued, "One of us has to stay here. It's definitely a crime scene made to look like an accident. There are no prints on anything that the victim should have had his prints on. Someone wiped everything off, even off the tub nozzle. If it was an accident, Lenny's prints would have been all over the bathroom and the tub." There was still no response from Steve. Bret proceeded to point out the facts of the crime. "Whoever did this made the mistake of cleaning up too well."

Steve finally responded to his partner. "I'll go; it looks like you're doing OK here." Steve glanced back at Rob Johnson, then back to Bret. "Look after him, will you? He doesn't look so good."

"I'll keep you updated"

"Yea, I'll call when I find anything." Steve headed towards their car.

XXXXX

Steve drove slowly, perhaps too slowly, towards Janice & Vivian's house. *Janice and Vivian, best friends.* He thought about it. *Vivian's boyfriend gets murdered, and Janice somehow knew about it either before or while it was happening . . . could this be some kind of twisted jealousy scheme?* In Steve's mind, Janice just knew a little too much about the murders. *Could the murders be connected?* He arrived at Vivian's house & slowly walked up to the front door. He didn't quite know why he was so apprehensive about questioning her. Perhaps it was because he did want to ask her questions, just not necessarily questions that related to the murder.

Vivian opened her front door. She smiled at the officer standing in front of her. She was sure that this was the enigmatic man that was quickly scampering away with her best friend's heart. "Well, Steve, what a pleasant surprise," she happily stated as she gradually began to notice the distressed look on his face. "What brings you here?" Looking around, she added, "Is Janice with you?"

"I'm afraid not. Not today, Vivian." Steve shifted uncomfortably. "Vivian, do you have a few minutes?"

Anticipation rose within Vivian. Her stomach began to roll inside. Thoughts raced through her head as she immediately wondered, *did Lenny tell Steve about his suspicions with Sharon's murder?* "Is this about Sharon Surf?" she blurted out without evaluating what she was saying, "because she's not really Joshua's sister." *Why did I just say that?* Vivian suddenly felt herself begin to perspire as she laid one hand on her stomach and the other on her forehead. "I don't feel so good, Steve. . . ."

Steve, observing Vivian's sudden flush, laid his hand under her elbow & led her toward her couch. "I'm sorry, Vivian, I didn't mean to startle you. Maybe you'd better sit down." How was he supposed to tell her now about her boyfriend's death? He suddenly found himself in a very bewildering situation. He somehow felt guilty for being there with her, and unexpectedly found himself wishing he had taken the option to let Brett take this chore. "Look, I need to tell you something." He heard the words coming out of his mouth but felt unaware of speaking them. "It's Lenny. He's . . . well, I understand you had a relationship with him?" Steve just couldn't seem to bring himself to tell her that her boyfriend was dead.

"Yea. I know he has some crazy ideas about Josh and Sharon, but that's all they are, ideas." She sat upright on the couch, the sweat beginning to dissipate. "I'm sorry, Steve, I don't know what came over me."

"Maybe you're psychic like your friend," he sarcastically stated, beginning to feel agitated himself.

"Oh, no, definitely not anything like Janice." A smile cut across her face. "But really, Steve, sometimes he just comes up with some crazy ideas—Lenny, that is. I mean, you really shouldn't take what he says seriously. He just—"

"Vivian," Steve cut her off abruptly, "that's not what I'm here about." He looked around. "Do you want something to drink?"

"Are you coming onto me?"

"No." He began to feel insulted. "I mean, water or something."

"I'm just kidding, silly; I know you're dating Janice."

"Am I?" A small feeling of enchantment began to creep up somewhere deep within Steve. Then obscurity emerged as he remembered the situation he was in and what he had to tell Vivian. "Look, Vivian, I have to ask you something."

"OK, shoot."

"You and Janice met with Sharon for lunch on Wednesday, am I correct?"

"Yes." Vivian began to feel a little uncomfortable at the way Steve was speaking to her. It seemed to her that he wasn't one hundred percent focused, and he constantly had a distressed look on his face. "Well, actually, no. She was supposed to meet us, but something came up."

"Where was that exactly?"

"It was this Mexican place we liked, right down the street."

"Did she say why she couldn't make it?" *Am I stalling,* he wondered to himself. He asked Vivian about the small details that couldn't possibly lead him to a conclusion about either case.

"No, she just left a note with the guy at the door." Vivian suddenly stopped herself and looked into Steve's eyes. *Why is he asking me about this?* A sudden concern swept over her, and she felt as if her stomach was going to explode. "Why?"

Despite the uncomfortable state of mind he was in, Steve immediately reverted his thoughts to the case at hand and of the torn piece of paper with Sharon's handwriting on it in Joshua's home. His entire stance changed almost instantaneously. He was sitting up, leaning forward, amd eagerly looking into Vivian's eyes. "What was written on the note, exactly?"

"I don't know." She shifted backwards. "Steve, this is not a good time. Do you think—"

"Vivian, this is important. Was anyone else with you and Janice at the restaurant?" He took both of her hands in his, needing her to understand the importance of his question. "Can you remember anything about the note?"

Vivian composed herself and promptly pulled her hands out of his grasp. "I told you I don't remember!" Facing Steve, she stood up, petulance slowly rose inside of her. "Really, Steve, if we could do this another time, I'd really appreciate it."

Steve's head dropped. He looked so vulnerable on her couch, so distressed. She felt guilt creep its way up her spine as she looked at the officer that could very well be "the one" for her best friend. She leaned over and put her hand on his shoulder. "I'm sorry; I just don't feel too well. Maybe the weather is getting to me." *What could be making him so incredibly disheartened,* she wondered. *Could it be that Janice turned him down?* "Look, Steve, all I know is that me, Janice and Josh were supposed to meet Sharon for lunch. She backed out, and Josh didn't show." She re-composed herself as Steve looked up at her.

"Joshua Surf was supposed to meet you guys?" he asked her as he stood up.

"Yea, but, I don't know, maybe he was just late. Maybe he came by after we left or something." Smiling again, Vivian looked nothing like the weak lady he watched almost pass out in front of him.

"What about the note? Where is it?"

"We left it with the doorman. Maybe Josh got it when he arrived asking for Sharon's party" She walked toward her kitchen, obviously feeling better. "Would you like something to drink?"

"So it was a cancellation note," Steve probed on. *Clearly Vivian is feeling better,* he noted as he tried to help recollect her memory of the note. "Something to the effect of . . . 'Sorry for the inconvenience. . . . '"

Vivian, standing in front of her open refrigerator, spun around with a Coke in her hand. "Yea, something to that effect. You like Coke?" she asked, handing him the soda.

XXXXX

Brett wasn't sure that Rob should be alone at a time like this, but Rob had insisted on leaving the crime scene in order to "grieve" for his son the way he felt he should. As the forensics crew dusted the place over and came to their conclusions, Brett stood outside facing Lenny's home. The yard was large, and the vast trees and modest sidewalk out in front of the house made the area look pleasant and welcoming. Cars drove by, slowing as they passed Lenny's house to gawk at the sight of police vehicles, the ambulance, and the vans that accommodated the investigating crew. One of the various cars pulled into the driveway. Brett began walking towards the vehicle, ready to direct the spectator back to the road when he recognized the driver.

"Janice, what are you doing here?" he asked, walking to her open window.

"I wanted to talk to Lenny." She apprehensively looked around at the crime scene. "Brett, where's Steve? What's going on?"

"I think you should just go on home. Vivian will need a friend. . . ."

"Why, what's happened?" Janice felt a rush of anxiety sweep into her as Brett attempted to dissuade her from opening the car door. She resolutely opened the driver side door and got out of her car. "Brett, tell me what's going on; why would Vivian need me at home?"

"Look, Janice, something terrible has happened. I need to ask you some questions."

"OK, but you have to tell me what's going on here."

"I will, I promise, but please, I need you to help me."

"Fine, what do you need to know?" She hesitantly walked closer to the house as he strode next to her.

"Look, Janice, Lenny's been murdered. His father found him here."

"What?" Horror overcame her. She rapidly felt a deep sense of loss and empathy for her friend. "When? How?" Words seemed to evade her. She had so many questions but couldn't seem to put a single sentence together.

"It was just this morning when he found the body." Brett continued to explain to Janice how it was set up to look like a suicide but was indeed a homicide; perhaps a pre-conceived murder. Janice listened intently as she began to realize that Lenny had allegedly been murdered at essentially the same time she got her intense headache the day before. She wondered how she could have known that he was leaving this world. How could she have been linked to this man? She realized many years ago that her insights were simply something that she had to live with and perhaps would never understand. It still didn't stop her from wondering how she could stop something terrible from happening if she only got the notion at the exact time as the encounter. Her thoughts and curiosity began to take her away. Brett's voice seemed to be a distant thought. Her mind shifted back to the deep sound of his voice as he asked her about last week's meeting with Sharon.

"I just can't shake the feeling that they might be related." Brett noticed that Janice was drifting off. "The murders, I mean," he clarified as he made eye contact with her.

"I'm sorry; I guess my thoughts wandered off."

"That's ok, I understand." Continuing to look her in the eyes, he promptly realized what it was about this lady that made his partner lose all concentration.

"So, did you and Vivian meet Sharon this last Wednesday for lunch?"

"We were supposed to, but she didn't show up." Janice looked around Lenny's property, a sadness descending in her heart. "She left us a note saying that she couldn't make it."

"A note? What did it say?"

"I just told you." Janice turned to face Brett. "It said that she couldn't meet us."

"Was it just you and Vivian? Could someone else have gotten that note?"

"Why?" Janice felt irritated and confused as to why Brett would be asking her about a stupid note. "Are you avoiding the problem at hand? What about Lenny?"

"Janice, this is important. These two murders could be linked." Brett tried to make Janice understand that his intention was to get as much information that he could to work with, not to avoid the problem at hand. "Was anyone else with you that day?"

"No, just me and Vivian . . . sorry."

"No one else was supposed to meet you there?"

"I told you already, no one was there." Janice remembered that Joshua originally was going to meet them, but then discarded his responsibilities on Vivian at the last minute, as usual.

"You think Joshua Surf has something to do with this, don't you?" Janice turned to look at Brett. "I almost forgot, he was supposed to meet us there, but he never showed."

"What did the note say?"

"You're wasting your time, Brett. Joshua didn't write the note." She continued striding slowly around the front yard of Lenny's house. "It said something about her having 'official business' to take care of, just the kind of dimwitted comment that obviously came from Sharon. The doorman gave it to us . . . Sharon got it to him somehow. Josh never even showed."

"We'll see about that." Brett felt positive that he had his killer. The note that Joshua used for his alibi was the note that would ultimately convict him of being a brutal killer. Sharon did indeed write the note; the handwriting experts had already established that fact. Joshua must have waited until the girls left the restaurant, then went in on his own and retrieved the note to later use for his own alibi. All he needed to do now was to find a witness that could put Joshua Surf at the restaurant Thursday night.

XXXXX

Steve felt reluctant to take the soda from Vivian, but politely accepted it as she walked closer toward him & laid it in his hand.

"Vivian, I really need to tell you something." Feeling uncomfortable, he reached out his hand to her. "I really think you should sit down for this."

A resilient feeling of concern overcame Vivian as she slowly sat down on her couch, still keeping eye contact with the officer. "If this is about Sharon's death, I've already told you all that I know."

"It's not about Sharon, Vivian. It's about Lenny."

"You think he did it?"

"No, no, not at all." Steve felt his heart sink in his chest as he looked into Vivian's apprehensive brown eyes. Just as he took a seat beside her, there was a knock at the door. *Not now,* Steve thought. A stirring restlessness overcame his emotions.

"Let me get that." Vivian hesitantly stood up, still looking directly at Steve, and walked toward the door.

XXXXX

Bret arrived at the Italian restaurant less than ten minutes after he'd left the crime scene on Lenny's property. The parking lot looked practically empty. He figured that this particular restaurant was one that became more popular for the lunch crowd or as the night approached. He walked through the doors and was almost immediately greeted by the tall Mexican doorman. He explained who he was and inquired about the past Wednesday afternoon, and the meeting that was supposed to have taken place between Vivian, Janice, and Sharon.

"I understand Sharon Surf had left a note for her party?" he asked the man. "Two girls and a man were supposed to meet her that afternoon, am I correct?" He figured he'd add Joshua into the mix to see if he had, in fact, shown that night.

"Yes, sir," the tall man with the strong accent answered. "She had a taxi-cab drop off the message and a note that she had written for them."

"A cab?"

"Yes, she does this much; every month she have different messengers if she not make it."

"So they meet here often?"

"Yes, Mister Surf has good credit tab here."

"Was he here to meet her?"

"No, I figure he with Miss Sharon." Obviously the door man was trying to relay all the information to Bret that he could remember. "The other two show and I give them the note. They did stay to eat."

"So you gave them the note from the cab?"

"Yes sir, Officer."

"And Joshua Surf never showed?"

"No with the other two, no sir."

"Could he have showed up later?"

"I do not know. I leave at one o'clock, is end of my shift." He looked around the restaurant and used his arm to gesture across the room. "There still many people eating at that time. They come and go to the bar, but I clean up and leave at one. They no need me after that."

"So he could have come and gone without anyone noticing?"

"Yea, sure."

"Thanks for your time. I appreciate it." Bret handed the man a business card. "If anyone remembers anything, give me a call, OK?"

"Yes, thank you."

Bret turned and left the restaurant. As he got into his car and pulled out of the strip mall, he felt confident that he had the right guy. Joshua Surf must have gone by the restaurant after the girls left. He would have slipped in, took the note, and then used the genuine, hand-written note from Sharon as his alibi. *He sure didn't think this out too well,* Bret thought. He decided that Josh was simply a hasty thinker; he didn't factor in the small detail that the police would undoubtedly find out about the note, and that they would directly connect it back to him. It seemed apparent to Bret that Joshua Surf was a sloppy criminal. *Or maybe he was too immaculate?* It suddenly occurred to Bret that Josh Surf could just be a *bad* criminal; not too clean, not too sloppy, simply *bad* at being a criminal. Lenny's murder had to somehow be linked to Sharon's. Joshua's over-cleaning of the crime scene could lead to his defeat as thy linked him to both murders. *What was his motive?* Bret wondered. He thought of Sharon—*or rather Elizabeth*—and Joshua's relationship, and tried to figure out how Lenny factored into all of this.

XXXXX

"Mr. Johnson, what are you doing here?" Vivian asked as she opened the door to find Lenny's father on her front porch.

"Rob." Steve immediately jumped up from the couch and walked towards him. "What are you doing here, Rob? I thought you were staying with Brett."

Vivian, confused as to why Lenny's dad would be a suspect in Sharon's murder, looked at Steve quizzically. "Why would Mr. Johnson be with Brett?" She looked back at the distressed-looking man standing outside. "Would you care to come in?"

Rob, disheartened, looked up at Vivian's charming eyes. "I just thought maybe we could comfort each other," he feebly stated. "After all, he's told me so much about you. Am I correct in assuming that we both loved him?"

Vivian sharply looked at the officer behind her. "What's he talking about, Steve?"

Steve looked down at the wooden floor. "Vivian, I was trying to tell you."

"You haven't told her yet?" Rob asked, astonished.

"Told me what?" Vivian irritably inquired. "What's going on?"

Steve put his hand on Vivian's shoulder once again. "Vivian, I really think you should sit down."

"I don't want to sit down!" She boorishly yanked his hand off of her arm and turned to face Rob. "What's going on? Tell me!"

"It's Lenny," Rob exclaimed as tears began to fall from his bloodshot eyes. "Someone's killed him."

Vivian's mind didn't immediately register what Rob had just stated. She simply stared at the demure man in front of her. Steve stood behind her, unbelievingly looking at Rob's open display of devastation. Suddenly, Vivian's knees seemed to collapse as her body fell down and backwards onto Steve. He caught the limp body, lifting & moving her toward the couch. "Rob, why did you just blurt it out like that?"

"She asked for the truth, I just told her what she needed to know."

"Yea, well, you coulda been a little more subtle about it!"

"Why? Won't change the facts." Rob's face was flushed and swollen.

As Steve looked into the anguished man's eyes, he felt an overwhelming degree of sympathy ascend inside of him. "I'm sorry, Rob. You're right, but she's probably gonna be just as upset as you are when she wakes up." He looked from Rob to Vivian, then back to Rob again. "Help me out, will you?" He stood up after arranging her in a lying position on her couch. "She's in shock."

xxxxx

The short man stuttered as he spoke to Bret. Standing outside of the police station, he attempted to assist the officer by answering his questions. The language barrier seemed to dismay him as he told Bret about the delivery of the note the past Wednesday. He explained, as best he could, how the beautiful lady asked him to deliver a note she had written from the airport to a restaurant in the suburbs. She had given him cash—the amount of what would be the cab fee—plus a noteworthy amount more as a tip for his trouble.

"She say she cannot leave airport for some emergency." The cab driver stumbled over the words he was attempting to project to the officer. "I tell her, lady—why you no just call? Is less money." He shook his head and lifted his hand to his head. "I no understand, but I do what she asks. She gives me address, I go."

"So you drove a note from the airport to the restaurant here?" Bret wanted to be sure that he clearly understood what took place that afternoon before he made any arrests or accusations. "And you handed the note to . . . whom?"

"I give the note to the man at the door," he put his hands out slightly, "and I leave."

"OK, thanks for your help. I appreciate you coming out here." Bret jotted a few notes in his notepad as the cab driver began to open his driver's side door.

"It's not a problem. I am out here anyhow." The man got into his car, windows all down, and shut the door. "I hope I do help you."

"Yes, you did. Thanks again." Bret turned and walked toward the station, taking note that both the cab driver and the doorman's stories meshed. Same times, same statements. They also were in sync with Janice's statement. The only story that didn't quite fit was Joshua Surf's. He needed to find Steve and see what he made of this whole mess. And what happened to the note? Maybe he could find the busboy from the restaurant. But what were the chances that the busboy would remember anything from that night, even if he could find him?

XXXXX

Holding a cold towel over Vivian's forehead, Rob continued to explain his point of view about his son's murder to the officer. The poor girl remained unconscious on the couch. He needed to know, beyond a doubt, that Steve understood how Lenny did not commit suicide but was brutally killed. It was absolutely mandatory that the police would look into this case as a first degree murder, and Rob wanted to help them find the hideous person who'd done this immoral act to his only son.

Vivian began to shift her position on the couch.

"Good, she's coming to," Rob stated, looking down at the pale girl.

"This time, try to be a little more subtle."

"Why? She already knows he's dead."

"She passed out. She's waking up, and she could be thinking it was all a dream."

"Not when she looks up and sees us both here again." Rob had a convincing point.

"Still, I just don't want to upset her any more." Steve felt inept, knowing that he could not do or say anything to change the facts of the matter. Vivian gradually opened her eyes. Regaining consciousness, she looked back and forth from Rob to Steve.

"What happened?" she inaudibly asked, feeling vulnerable and distressed as she looked up unsteadily into the two men's faces.

"Do you want some water?" Steve fretfully asked. Suddenly the memories began to come back to Vivian. She began to remember Rob's disheartening words to her, about Lenny being, *(could it have possibly been a dream?)* dead. Anxiety overwhelmed her once again, but this time the blood rushing throughout her head did not get the chance to take over. She stood up, leaving the two dismal-looking men sitting on her couch. "Lenny, where is he?" she demanded. "Is he at the hospital?"

"Vivian, I'm afraid he's gone." Steve tried to lay it on her as gently as possible. "It's true, I'm sorry."

"But I was just with him. I only just talked to him yesterday." She felt dismayed and delusional; nothing seemed to be solid or real around her. It was as if she was sitting on the outside looking in at her surroundings. Everyone and everything resembled a movie taking place right before her eyes. She had so much to ask, so many questions, but no words would escape her lips.

"Breathe, Vivian," she heard a voice saying as she felt someone lifting her. She noticed the color of the walls in her living room. She felt herself inhale and realized that she had been holding her breath for a while, but she didn't really care. In fact, nothing seemed to matter to her presently. All she could think about was the thickness in the air, and how the light color of paint suited the walls next to the large window on the opposite side of the room.

"No," she heard herself mutter. Voices surrounded her yet were absolutely incomprehensible. "No, it wasn't supposed to be Lenny," she continued to mutter. "He wasn't supposed to be involved at all." She looked up at the ceiling, then out at the lawn beyond the window. "He just misunderstood everything." Darkness began to welcome Vivian once again. She closed her eyes and simply wished to be wherever it was that Lenny now resided. "He left me here alone."

"Yea, she's definitely out of it." Rob held her head in his hand and placed it on the pillow to the side of the couch. He looked up at Steve, who seemed to be feeling not-so-hot himself. "I don't think she heard a word either one of us said there, Steve."

"No, you're right. This isn't good." He looked around the room, then back down at Vivian's still body. "I think we need to get her to a hospital."

"Or put her in her own bed," Rob presumed. "If she wakes up in a hospital it's gonna be even more disillusioning to her."

He had a point, but Steve didn't' want to leave her there alone. "Someone's got to stay with her." Just as he stood up, the front door opened. A surprised looking, familiar face stood in the doorway.

Chapter 19

Monday Evening

"What's everyone doing here?" asked Janice as she walked into her home. She expected it to be empty but found both Steve and Rob hovering over her feeble-looking, passed-out roommate. "What's going on?" She stepped into her house and closed the door behind her. Steve walked toward her, realizing how the scene would look confusing, and held his hand out to her.

"Janice, something's happened to Vivian's boyfriend."

"I know." She walked past Steve, disregarding his open hand, and headed toward her friend. "I already talked to Bret."

Baffled, Steve turned to face her. "What?"

"You heard me," she answered, not looking at him, but instead tending to her roommate. "He told me all about it."

"Are you ok?" He didn't quite know what to make of this new information he was hearing, but he was still surprised to see Janice taking the news so well, considering Vivian's reaction.

"Do I look ok?" She turned to face him. "Two people whom I knew personally have died—no, have been murdered—in not even a week. How am I supposed to be ok about that?"

"Sorry."

"You should be. Now will you please just go away and leave us alone?"

"Well, excuse me, but I am investigating these murders."

"What do you want from me?" Janice continued to prop Vivian's immobile head on a pillow. She seemed to become unmindful of any other person's presence in the room.

"Look, Janice, I know you're upset, but I need to ask you abut some things."

"Fine," she irritably stated. "What do you want to know?"

Steve shuffled nervously. He had her attention and her willingness to assist, but he couldn't figure out why she seemed so irritated at him. She had been through a lot, and he supposed that different people react in different ways. Maybe this was just her way of defending herself from any sort of vulnerability. *Or maybe,* he thought, *she really is involved in all of this mess.*

"Look, Janice, I don't really know exactly what I'm looking for from you."

"Are you talking about the cases or personally?" she replied in a vague tone.

Steve was surprised at the question. "Well, the case of course," he replied in a matter-of-fact manner. He didn't know what to say to her. He just stood there, stunned, and stared at her. She finally sensed that he was offended and realized that she was taking out all her anxiety on him simply because he was there.

"I'm sorry, Steve. I'm just not used to any of this."

He felt himself ease up. He even felt a little humor in the whole situation. "The cases or personally?" he heard himself saying aloud as he realized he might be pushing it a little.

Janice smiled as she stood up and walked in his direction. "Really, Steve, what do you want to know?"

He forced himself to refocus on the case and the missing pieces that he desperately needed to link.

"Saturday night we spoke to Joshua Surf." He shuffled through a notepad that he had pulled out of his back pocket. Holding the notepad in one hand, he lifted his other hand and rested it on his head. "He said that Sharon, er—Elizabeth, had left a note for him on the door of the warehouse." He looked up at Janice, hand still rubbing lightly on his head. "Did you see a note taped to the door Thursday night before you left, or maybe after?"

Steve looked bewildered to Janice. She started to feel compassion for him as she realized he probably hadn't had much sleep in the last few days.

"I didn't see any note taped to the warehouse, or in it for that matter, sorry." Janice felt bad that she could do nothing to help him. She thought she might try to help him process the information that he already had into a more clear understanding of what he was looking for. The way she knew how to do that best was to get him to talk about it.

"What did it say?"

"It just said something—that she was sorry she couldn't make it, official business to take care of . . ." He was ready to tell her his theory about Josh going into the restaurant after the girls had left; that he thought Josh went in and took the note that they'd left on the table and then used that note as an alibi. He just needed to link the notes—to get some proof that it was in fact the same note. He looked at Janice, ready to talk to her, when he noticed the shocked look in her eyes.

"What's the matter, Janice?" He quickly approached her, both arms reaching out to her. "Do you know something I should know?"

Rob loomed closer to the couple, observing each passage and every lingering body language movement taking place.

"That note," Janice mumbled, deep in thought, "that's the one Sharon left for us Wednesday afternoon." A look of realization appeared on her face as she looked from Steve to Rob, then back to Steve again. "Vivian . . ." she began to say. She stopped herself and looked at her roommate, who was still knocked out from the shock of Lenny's death. Janice shut her mouth instantly and directed her attention to her best friend.

"Are you sure it's the same note?" Steve felt a revitalization of hope ascend within him despite all the horror and destruction around him. He was positive that he had the killer now. Joshua Surf must have gone in after the girls left, taken the note from the table where they left it, and torn the bottom off of the note; the part that was specifically meant for Vivian and Janice. He used that note the following night as his alibi, knowing that it was indeed Sharon's handwriting. He must have realized that fact would prove true as the investigation proceeded. He also linked Vivian's statements about how Lenny knew that Joshua was the killer. Josh must have disposed of Lenny in order to have no witnesses. Lenny must have had evidence for Joshua to go to such lengths to cover himself.

"Vivian's coming to," he heard Janice saying. "I think you should give us some space." She looked up at Steve and Rob. "She'll need some time with this."

Rob smiled dutifully. "I suppose you're right. She's not taking this too well."

"I'm so sorry for your loss," Janice sympathetically said to Rob. She realized that he had just experienced a loss greater than her friend; he'd lost his son. "I didn't even offer you anything to drink."

"No, no need for any of that," Rob kindly answered. "I'll be heading out. You take care of her." Directing the conversation toward the officer, he stated, "Good luck. Keep me posted, will you?"

"Sure will, thanks," Steve compassionately answered Rob.

"Thank you."

Janice looked at Steve as Rob turned and headed toward the door. "Should he be alone right now?"

"He'll be fine." Steve looked at Vivian, who appeared to be slowly waking up, then back to Janice. "That note . . . I know what the top said, the part Joshua tore off, but what did the bottom say?"

"Joshua tore off?"

"Yea, the note he had—the bottom was torn off." He explained the facts of the case to Janice, along with his theory of how and why Joshua murdered both victims. She seemed dismayed at the entire situation, yet seemed to understand and agree with his theories. He felt a feeling of both guilt and relief as he became confidence that Janice had nothing to do with either of the murders, but something still seemed to be missing. He would have to talk to his partner about the situation and find out what information Bret had.

XXXXX

Bret and Steve decided to meet at the coffee shop. There was nothing like caffeine late in the day to keep their minds sharp.

"It was five days ago. How could he be sure?" Steve asked his partner.

"He can't, but he seemed pretty convinced. He said that he would have noticed a note in case some 'pretty lady' left him her number." With a coy grin on his face, he added, "Like that's common. You shoulda seen this guy."

"Not quite the lady's man, huh?"

"Not even close."

"So they could have left it at the front, or it could have fallen under the table." Steve found himself covering every possibility to keep his suspicion of Janice diminished. "Just because no one found the note on the table just after they left doesn't mean that one of them kept it."

"No, it doesn't," Bret agreed. "In fact, I think it's safe to say we're on the same page with convicting Josh."

They continued to compare notes about the victims and the cases; how they linked, motive, facts, and theories they each had. It seemed very clear to both of them that they had their man.

"Well, I guess we need to make an arrest," Bret verified after a couple hours of discussion with his partner, and over way too many cups of coffee and tea.

"Yea," Steve agreed, "I think we just have to make one more stop on the way."

XXXXX

As they pulled into the parking lot of Find-U Corporation, Bret filled Steve in on his findings about the Surf family history from Pam Lily at the adoption agency.

"So, you think this 'Officer Rose' can help us?" he asked Steve.

"Well, she's been looking into Vivian's life for her, and apparently, Josh and Vivian are related."

"Crazy." They stepped out of the car and headed toward the front door of the large brick building. As they walked into the neutrally decorated office building, they almost immediately noticed the flamboyant lady. She was cleaning up her desk and humming lightly to herself. She looked up toward them, still humming, as a smile emerged from her face. She laid the pile of papers that she was holding down and began to walk towards them.

"Well, hello. I was wondering if you two were going to make it before I took off." Her jolly voice echoed in a light-hearted manner. "You do realize I had to ok this with Miss Vivian. It is her life you're looking into, after all," she bluntly stated. Her hand reached out to shake each of the officers'.

"Yes, of course," Bret replied as he shook her hand. "I'm Bret, and this is my partner, Steve." They each shook her hand and said their hellos. Steve went on to explain to the kind lady that they were working on a case that involved some of the facts that she'd uncovered during her pursuit of Vivian's birth-family.

"I understand that you found out Joshua Surf is Vivian's birth-brother?" Steve asked at the conclusion of his explanation.

"Yes, well, I think I gave her a bit of a shock on that one," Sara embarrassingly admitted as she fanned at her face with a loose sheet of paper. "You see, I just assumed that she'd known; after all, she does work for him!" She looked from one face to the other, hoping to get some positive feedback on the situation. Neither officer seemed to make an issue out of the misunderstanding.

"But, you know," she continued after she received no contrite reaction, "the poor girl was so stunned to find out about Joshua being her brother that I never did get around to telling her the good news!" Her smile widened and she looked extremely proud of herself. She just stood in front of the men with a pleased look on her face until one of them finally spoke.

"And what was the good news, Ms . . ." Bret began to ask.

"Oh, please, call me Sara."

"OK, Sara, so . . . the good news was?"

"Oh, yes." Sara snapped back to reality. "The inheritance." The smile emerged once again. "Vivian's biological parents left her a nice piece of land with a very significant-sized house on the lot when they passed—"

"Hold on; Vivian Shlimon owns that house?" Steve intervened. "The one on 57th Street in Chicago?"

"Why, yes." Sara looked perplexed. "It seems I'm just completely off this week. When I assume someone knows something, they don't, and when I think they need an explanation, they don't, either!" She began to babble on about her misinterpretation of information she'd acquired, and how she really needed to get on the ball. Bret interceded on her conversation with herself.

"Look, Ms. Officer Rose." He cut his thought short. "Why the officer prefix? Are you a state licensed . . ." For lack of a better word, he ended his thought, "Something?"

"Well," Sara began to explain in her merry way, "If the 'Geek Squad' from those computer stores can drive around in police getup and carry a cute little badge, why can't we be 'Officers of Justice' and 'Reunite-ation Officers' of families?" Her large smile and satisfied look were enough to make Bret wish he never asked the question in the first place.

"The land," he reverberated back to his original question, "does Vivian know it belongs to her?"

"I was trying to tell you," Sara persisted. "She was very shaken up about learning her family roots."

"And Joshua Surf must know who his long-lost sister is," Steve supposed aloud, speaking more to himself than those around him.

"Which means he lied to us about trying to find the sister he'd put up for adoption so many years ago." Bret finished his partner's thought. "I knew he was a rat."

"So why has he continued to pay the taxes all these years?" Steve and Bret were speaking to each other, but the enthusiastic lady in their midst interjected. "Well, isn't it obvious?"

Both officers turned, obviously perplexed, and faced her.

"Because Sharon Surf lives there." She took note of the puzzled looks on their faces as they looked at each other and back to her. She concluded that she'd done it again—assumed that they knew something that they didn't. Her grin drooped as she turned and headed towards a large file cabinet behind her desk. "Oh, it's right here. I have all the documentation; let me show you," she blandly stated while digging through the different slots.

✗✗✗✗✗

As they drove away from Find-U corporation and toward Joshua Surf's place in the city, both officers agreed that Joshua was the killer, but they still couldn't figure out what was going

113

on with that old house. Why had Josh paid just to keep it there? Just by visiting, it was more than evident that no one could possibly reside there. But legally, Sharon Surf—*the real Sharon Surf*—had been living there for over ten years.

"Could anyone really live in that kind of atmosphere?" Bret wondered vocally to his partner. "I guess it would explain why her car was there."

"No way," Steve answered. "No one is living there. Someone drove that car and left it there to get rid of any indication that Elizabeth was still in Illinois".

"Makes sense; had to be Josh."

"No one else has a motive like that guy."

XXXXX

Vivian felt devastated as she sat on the couch next to Janice. She felt as if her life had been completely turned around, and she let all her emotions flow to her friend.

"First I find out that Josh is my brother; now the only man whom I thought I could have a relationship with is taken from me by Joshua." Tears swelled up in her eyes once again and she reached for another tissue.

"We don't know that, Vivian. It just looks that way." Janice tried to ease her friend's mind by stating an obvious fabrication. She wanted so badly to ease her friend's soul, but she didn't know how to do so. Vivian's tears began to subside as she calmed herself down.

"It just isn't fair," she mumbled to herself. "I only just find out that Josh is my brother, and now they're going to haul him off to prison for killing my boyfriend." Tears once again began to flow.

The phone rang, relieving Janice from her unsuccessful attempts to comfort Vivian. She picked up the phone to hear a welcome voice ask her how Vivian was doing.

"As well as can be expected, Steve. Thank you for calling." Janice held the conversation for a few minutes with the man she felt such adoration for. She still kept an eye on her roommate, hoping she would feel better.

"Are you sure?" Vivian heard her roommate promptly ask

the person on the other end of the phone line. "All of it? To Vivian?"

"What?" Viv asked.

Janice laid her hand on Vivian's arm, motioning for her to hold on while she cleared up the facts in her head. She tried to contemplate what she was hearing from Steve about Vivian inheriting a lot of land that was very valuable. Vivian suddenly reverted back to her conversations with Sara Rose earlier in the week. She realized that she must have been so baffled about finding out that Joshua Surf was her birth-brother that she completely overlooked talking to the nice lady about the property that she had tried to tell her about.

"OK, I'll let her know. Thank you, Steve." As she hung up the receiver, Janice couldn't seem to restrain the diminutive smile that emerged from her lips. A small amount of hope filled her heart as she turned to her friend and expressed that she owned a large plot of land with a mansion on it somewhere downtown Chicago. She explained that, when her parents died, they had left it in Vivian's name.

Vivian felt surprised, enchanted, and enraged all at the same time. She couldn't believe that she had such a grand fortune given to her as a gift from her birth parents. Yet she felt infuriated that her own blood-brother would keep information such as this from her. She suddenly realized why he never let her know who she really was; why he kept it all to himself. *How malicious,* she thought to herself as infuriation arose within her. He had taken everything that belonged to her—even her own identity! She would never forgive him for this outrage. A feeling of retribution came over her as she thought about how he would spend the rest of his life behind bars. She only wished that she would have somehow lead the police to him before he took dear Lenny away from her. If only she would have went to them as soon as Lenny admitted his suspicions to her about Joshua. *If only I would have put my feelings for Josh aside, I could have saved Lenny's life,* she regrettably thought. How could she have been so blind and naive? To think she was in love with her own brother. *If only I knew . . .*

"I have to find my sister," she heard herself say to Janice. "She's out there somewhere. He must know where she is. He's just keeping her in the dark like he did with me."

"Who?"

"Josh." Vivian cleared her thoughts. "Joshua lied to me. He knew all along that I was his sister. He must know where our other sister—the real Sharon—is." She looked up desperately into her friend's eyes. "Please help me find her. She's the last of my birth-family . . . my last hope."

XXXXX

Joshua was evidently enraged this time. *Those dense cops; don't they know when to give up?* He angrily pushed the button to speak. "What do you want now?" he harshly asked over the intercom.

"We just need to ask you one more thing, Josh," came the inconsiderate voice over the speaker. "You mind buzzing us up?"

"Actually, I do mind," answered an irritated Josh. "I think I've answered enough of your stupid questions. Now leave me alone." He turned to walk back to his kitchen, and then re-thought his path. He turned back and pushed the button once more. "This is called harassment, you know," he added. The officers couldn't help but notice how different his tone with them was this time. He seemed like an overgrown boy throwing a tantrum.

"Come on, Josh," they persisted on his speaker. "This will only take a minute. Then we'll be out of your hair forever."

"You promise?" Joshua cynically asked, leaning on the wall.

"You have my word," responded the coy voice on the other end. Joshua hesitantly buzzed the annoying officers up. "Fine. One minute."

As Joshua opened the door at their relentless pounding, he couldn't fight the horrendous fury growing inside him. Mentally and logically, he knew that he could not give in to his rage, but physically his body needed to explode. His mind wanted to demolish these insistent insects that kept him from unleashing his true potential.

"What do you want?" he pompously asked the officers, anger rising within him; his self-control peaking on the edge of insanity.

"Well, Josh" Bret stated, pushing his way into the room past the scrawny man, "it looks like we caught you in a big fat lie." He turned to face the pathetic man.

"What do you have to say to that, Josh?" Steve continued Bret's thought.

Joshua stared long and hard into each man's eyes. His back straightened, and he suddenly looked a lot larger than either officer remembered. Steadily, Josh got the words out of his mouth. "I told you everything you wanted to know. What do you believe I lied about today?"

There was definitely a change in Joshua Surf's entire demeanor, and Steve didn't like it. He coyly positioned his hand where he could easily pull his pistol out if needed. It was obvious to Steve that Bret felt the same change in the atmosphere. Steve answered the unsettling man, "Vivian Shlimon is your sister. That's why you gave her a job."

It was silent for a moment. Joshua looked deep into Steve's eyes and finally, after thirty seconds or so, answered the officers accusation. "So I wanted to protect her." He then looked over into Bret's eyes in the same manner. "You got a problem with people tryin' to take care of their families?"

Un-intimidated, Bret glared back at the appalling man and pompously answered him. "If taking care of means murdering, yea, I got a problem with that."

Without warning, Joshua reached into his sports jacket and retrieved a large knife. The rage overcame him; he could no longer hold in the anger he'd so carefully contained over the years. He swiftly ran toward the officer who'd accused him of killing the only woman he'd ever known to be worthy of his love. Steve's instantaneous reaction was expert. He pulled his trigger and hit Joshua straight through the heart. He fell, first looking unbelievingly at Steve, then down at the blood beginning to run through his neatly pressed shirt. The knife remained tightly in his hand. Realization came upon him. He knew that he was about to die, yet he could feel no physical pain. He knew that he'd lost control in the midst of these depraved men who lived only to destroy genuine brilliance. He knew that he'd let out his true conduct; deep down, they only feared him. He'd held his anger in so brilliantly over the years. He was going to be truly great some day. Now the world would have to go on without his immaculate wisdom, all because these two foolish nuisances couldn't let it go. He refused to die feebly as he stared deep into each officer's eyes. Then the great darkness came to encompass all that he once was; the entirety of all that he should have been allowed to be. He made one last request as he honorably closed his eyes without complaint. "The house," he clearly stated. "Leave the house alone."

Chapter 20

Tuesday Morning

Back at the breakfast café, Steve and Bret reminisced about the events that had taken place the night before. Bret still wanted to take the house apart and find out why Joshua's last request was to leave it standing. But Steve believed that, under all his psychotic behavior, Josh might be a little compassionate in his own way. Maybe it was a symbol to him; perhaps the house stood as a representation of what Joshua's family might have been to him.

"Yea, that's all good and dandy there, Steve," Bret said after listening to his partner's optimistic rambling about finding some kind of good inside a hapless assassin. "But, personally, I don't respect the last requests of murdering criminals." He stuffed a large bite of his breakfast in his mouth and continued with his point. "The way I see it, we go tear that eye sore down and see what he's hiding in there."

"Well, even if we wanted to, we gotta get permission from Vivian—it's her land."

"It's a crime scene."

"No crime was committed there, Bret."

"We won't know that until we tear it down and find out what the scumbag's hiding." Bret seemed fixed on this issue, and Steve admitted to himself that his partner had a solid point.

"Fine." Steve surrendered to his partner's argument. "I'll

explain the situation to Vivian and get her permission." He looked at Bret and genuinely affirmed, "But she might not go for it. Bret, this is her only link to any blood relatives she has, you know."

"I know, and as soon as we find her sister, she'll be happy to give up that old disaster sitting on her property."

XXXXX

Steve and Bret had gathered a squad to come out to the mansion in Chicago with them. They'd hired some wreckers, and Vivian had not shown any emotional attachment to the house nor the property. She signed the papers stating that the police could do whatever they felt necessary to the house in order to convict the late Joshua Surf of any and every possible crime he might have committed. Steve did find it rather peculiar that Vivian wanted such an intense amount of retribution toward someone who was not only deceased, but also her blood relative—the only one she knew at this point in her life. Steve had spoken to Janice about the situation earlier, and she too felt that Vivian was taking it a step overboard with the vindication toward Josh. But they both agreed that it must be natural to feel a fair amount of hatred toward someone who'd lied to her all his life. Affection and sympathy would come with time. For now, Vivian's desire for revenge worked out well for the police, who were looking for more reason to convict the deceased slaughterer.

The crew worked adamantly at going through the mansion. Steve did take note of its magnificence one last time. It must have truly been an immaculate residence in its day. He still could not understand why psychotic Josh would let it rot away like this. Even the foundation had been built sturdily. It still held the entire estate solidly. He was a little embarrassed to admit to himself that he was a sap for magnificence, but he hated to see such an estate torn down. No builder in this day and age would ever build a place with that much stamina there again. It was truly a shame.

Steve snapped back to reality as he noticed many of the people working on the site rapidly proceeding toward the hallway area. At first, as he walked closer to the crowd, he didn't comprehend what everyone was gathering around. As he proceeded closer to the incensed crowd, he began to understand what was going on.

"The entire body is here." He heard one voice, then another. "Who did this guy think he was, Joseph Stallin?"

Similar sentences emerged. "Well, at least he left the bodies in tact," he'd hear one person stating. "Yea, no heads cut off or anything." There were more conversations. Overwhelming realizations defeated Steve as he found his way to his partner and confirmed the ghastly convictions about Joshua swimming through his mind. He'd murdered his entire family, sparing only Vivian Shlimon—for whatever reason. And he gave her away to a family he'd never have to meet. *What kind of a ludicrous person would do this to his own family?* Unfortunately for Steve, he had the privilege of meeting these kinds of people all the time.

Chapter 21

Tuesday Afternoon

Back at the police station, Joshua Surf was officially convicted, dead or alive, of the brutal murders of five innocent people. If he were still alive, he would have been given the death sentence. His parents, legally declared dead so many years ago, their bodies never found, were assumed by the adoption agency to have left their children alone in the world to fend for themselves. Now, in new light of the situation, it was apparent that they had indeed been killed by their own ravenous, egotistic, selfish son, who used the abundance of money that he'd acquired from their wills to build his own ego into a fortress. His unfortunate sister, Sharon, must have refused to go along with his scheme, leaving him no choice but to kill her and leave her remains in the grand house alongside her beloved parents.

Everything added up: the house, Sharon supposedly residing there for so many years, the car left to rot with the house. *But why,* Steve thought, *did he kill Elizabeth?* There were a few missing links to the whole story, but with a man as psychotically twisted as Joshua turned out to be, who was Steve to question the reasoning of insanity?

XXXXX

Janice still couldn't believe all the proceedings that had gone on within the last week alone. As she sat in   Steve's favorite coffee shop across from him, she felt lucky, despite all the havoc taking place around her. She looked around the quaint coffee place and noticed that it was decorated much like a book store—very warm and homely.

"You come here a lot?" she asked him as he sat across from her, obviously staring. She felt her face begin to flush.

"What?"

"You." He gave her a warm smile.

"What about me?"

"You look nice," he answered for lack of better conversation at the moment. She smiled and looked down at her hands crossed on the table. He slowly placed his hands over hers from the other side and looked up at her. She didn't resist the display of affection.

"Thank you." She looked back at him. After a few long seconds of silence between them, she attempted to make conversation to keep from feeling so pleasantly awkward.

"I'll bet you're glad this is all over," she stated.

"Hopefully it is." His mood began to shift to dimmer thoughts as he began to explain to her how they came to the mutual conclusion that Joshua Surf was guilty of the multiple murders.

"So why do you say it's hopefully over?"

"You know, you gotta plan for the worst," he stated matter-of-factly.

"Not always." She smiled at him, bringing back feelings of pleasure inside him again. "So what was the link?"

"The link?" Baffled, he brought himself back to the disheartening conversation. "The link to the murders, you mean?"

She nodded in agreement. "Yea, you know, what brought the two together?"

"The note," he answered. He pushed aside any doubts about why she would want to know more about the cases. *She's just making conversation,* he thought as his hands began to unlock from hers and move back to his cup. *I'm talking to her about the case; of course she'll ask questions.*

"The note?" she repeated his answer back to him. "Really? Just the note?" She seemed distraught somehow. "Wow." She looked down at her coffee as she wrapped her hands around her cup.

"Yea, why?" He heard himself compulsively say, "I mean, why do you look so sad about it?" He corrected his harsh tone.

"It just seems like such a small detail." She looked back up at him. "I mean, what if he's innocent; is that the only thing you have to tie him to the murders?" She genuinely looked concerned about the presumption. "Everyone will remember him as such a terrible person, even if he didn't kill them."

Steve couldn't quite understand why this would bother her. Nevertheless, he explained to her that there were many other reasons to convict Joshua of both murders. For one, everything added up with his family and the estate. Lenny, from Vivian's testimony, had some reason to blackmail Josh; some proof to convict him. Everything tied together; the note was just the closing evidence. *Except,* Steve thought to himself, *why he would kill the girl he claimed to love?* Steve thought better of pointing his doubts out to Janice, especially the way she appeared to be defending the deceased killer.

"Besides," he added, "people are going to think badly of him anyway for what he did to his own family." He was referring to the bodies buried in the walls of the spectacular house.

"True . . ."

"What's on your mind?"

Janice loomed back to reality from the distant dream she had been contained in for previous last minute or so. "You're right, Steve," she contentedly supposed. "Let's not mess up our first real date with all this gloomy talk about cases you've already solved."

Real date, Steve thought. Although he already knew that they were on an official date, he enjoyed hearing the words that assured him he wasn't dreaming come from Janice's soft lips. A grin crept onto his face as he realigned his hands with hers across the coffee table.

"Sounds like a plan to me."

XXXXX

Vivian reassured Sara Rose that she had done nothing wrong in giving Steve and Bret any information they had asked for regarding her family history. In fact, she had been inquiring into the possibility of Ms. Rose doing even more investigative work into her brother's hidden life in order to dig up any other lies he might have concealed throughout the years.

"I told you already, they're working on a case to convict a very bad man. I want to do anything I can to help."

"But Vivian, dear," Sara softly affirmed, "he's already been convicted. And after all, he has moved on." Sara was trying to get a point across in her own delicate manner—that perhaps Vivian should let it go. Her brother was deceased, and maybe she should leave well-enough alone and let him rest in peace. She'd never seen a girl so full of hatred toward another human being; especially after just finding out that he was her brother.

"You don't understand, Sara." Tears began to fill the cups of her eyes. "If only I'd known, I could have saved Lenny." She looked down at her folded hands as Sara reached for a tissue on the table next to the couch. Viv gratefully took the tissue from the kind lady's hand and began to blot her eyes with it. "I think I loved him, but now I'll never get the chance to find out."

Sara placed her hand on Vivian's shoulder. "There, there, dear."

"I'm sorry." She sat upright again and folded the tissue in her hands.

"Don't be. It's only human to feel emotion." Sara felt a little relieved to see the affectionate side of this poor girl who'd been through so much in the last week. She began to understand that all of the anger and vengeance that had been coming from Vivian was just a cover-up for all the pain and loss she'd had to deal with in such a short time.

"I must say, dear," Sara continued, "that there is always a light somewhere in the darkness, no matter how diminutive that light may seem."

Getting a hold on her sniffing, Vivian, confused, looked at the lady sitting next to her. "What are you talking about?"

"Something called an inheritance, dear."

"You already told me about that house." Vivian felt agitated that Sara kept bringing up a house that had been ripped down and apparently been a burial ground for victims. "I would never live on that land after everything that's happened."

"No, not that inheritance." Sara smiled and placed her hand on Vivian's lower arm. "Joshua Surf, dear. You're his only living relative. You inherit everything."

Chapter 22

Tuesday Evening

One week had passed, but it seemed closer to a year for Janice and Vivian. As they sat together in their living room, Vivian flipped the channels on the remote control, keeping the mute button on.

Janice seemed more restless than she'd been in months. She stood up and roamed the house. She walked to and from the kitchen, but retrieved nothing from the refrigerator or any of the cabinets.

Silence thrived within the house.

"How was your lunch date?" Vivian asked her jittery friend.

"Fine." Janice placed herself on the sofa, facing her companion. Looking directly into her eyes, she asked Vivian the question that she had wanted to ask her for the last two days. "Why did you do it?"

They looked at each other in silence for over a minute. The air felt thick with remorse. Vivian only looked back at her friend remotely, no sign of regret on her face.

"What are you talking about?"

"The note, Vivian." Janice felt distressed, but her restlessness began to subside. "I saw you put it in your purse that night".

"I thought I loved him," she blandly stated. Her eyes began

to lower as her focal point fixed on the coffee table in front of her. "All these years of working for him . . . all this time . . . all lies."

"Why Sharon?"

"Elizabeth." Vivian, fuming, looked up at her friend again. "Her name was Elizabeth. He even made her lie for him!"

They both sat in silence for over a minute as Janice waited for Vivian to calm herself and continue. "Wednesday night, when her car was still at the warehouse, remember?"

"Yea, Josh was there too," Janice calmly stated.

"Right." Viv shifted in the couch. "I knew she was in there with him waiting until we left to go out to her car & drive back to her apartment. It all became so clear just then."

"That you had to kill her?"

"No." She looked up, an offended look on her face. "That she wasn't his sister; that he'd been playing all of us." The insulted look dissipated as she looked down again. "I was angry. And hurt."

"That's what that was," Janice stated in realization. "On likelihood of sounding bizarre, I think I felt your pain that night when we were in the office."

"Yea?" A small grin emerged from Vivian's face. "I knew you'd understand."

Janice felt heartbroken for her friend, for Sharon, for Lenny, and even for Joshua, living in that disturbing world of his own. "Look, I'm not saying that I understand or that it's OK to kill someone." Lost for words, she looked over at Vivian and saw that her friend's eyes were swelling up with tears.

"If I'd only know he was my brother . . ."

Janice stood up and moved to the grief-stricken girl as she continued to speak through her tears. "None of this would have happened and Lenny would still be alive." Sobs of despair flooded from Vivian as Janice moved the tissue box closer to them and handed her companion a tissue.

"It's going to be OK, Viv," she mumbled as she wrapped both arms around her. "You're going to get through this . . ."

XXXXX

As Janice sat alone in her room, she tried to clear her mind and decide what she needed to do. *Everyone has secrets,* she thought. *Everyone has longings and dreams of a better place.*

None of these wishes are necessarily bad. They become bad when the secrets turn into malicious murders and the longings turn into deep sinister desires; when the dreams turn into hopeless necessities. They become bad when love and hate become so closely integrated that a person can't really tell where one ends and the other begins.

Janice supposed that Joshua had every material item that he'd ever wanted. Whatever anyone could possible desire, he'd obtained . . . everything except peace of mind. Joshua Surf believed that money and power would alleviate him from the hand of justice. Maybe he was right; could still be.

Money and power have their place in this society. Joshua certainly knew that. Perhaps if he had been sentenced before his demise, he'd have softened up after he'd served his ten or fifteen years in prison for first-degree murder, his standing in society helping him out. Perhaps he would have hardened and become even more of a power-hungry beast. *Who's to say? Not me,* Janice thought, *not to his face, anyway. I sure wouldn't want to end up like Lenny—nothing left to say ever again.*

Janice's secret, if it was indeed a secret, would be that she loved Vivian, even after knowing the reality of what she did. Vivian made a mistake, either out of love or hate. Whichever way, the tie was pretty close. Joshua did a terrible thing, and he would somehow pay for that through reputation the rest of the days that his memory survived. *Joshua's reputation wouldn't become improved if one murder was taken off his list,* Janice realized. *After all, why should I attempt to modify convictions that have already been determined?*

The End

Tate Publishing, LLC

Tate Publishing is committed to excellence in the publishing industry. Our staff of highly trained professionals—editors, graphic designers, and marketing personnel—work together to produce the very finest book products available. The company reflects in every aspect the philosophy established by the founders based on Psalms 68:11, "The Lord gave the word and great was the company of those who published it."

If you would like further information, please call
1.888.361.9473
or visit our website at
www.tatepublishing.com

Tate Publishing LLC
127 E. Trade Center Terrace
Mustang. Oklahoma 73064 USA